PAIUTE PASSAGE

STONECROFT SAGA 11

B.N. RUNDELL

WOLFPACK
PUBLISHING
— EST 2013 —

WOLFPACK
PUBLISHING
— EST 2013 —

Paiute Passage

Paperback Edition
Copyright © 2020 B.N. Rundell

Wolfpack Publishing
6032 Wheat Penny Avenue
Las Vegas, NV 89122

wolfpackpublishing.com

Paperback ISBN 978-1-64734-180-0
eBook ISBN 978-1-64734-179-4

PAIUTE PASSAGE

DEDICATION

One of the most memorable times for any author is when someone reads their first book, and then asks, "When's the next one coming?" That simple question says volumes, and when it is asked time and again, it is wrapped in the package of encouragement that every author thrives on and seeks after. A kind word, a question of interest about the story or the characters, a positive review, are the things that keep the keyboards clattering and the hopes of the noisemaker high, anticipating a new reader or readers, so that the next book, if there is one, will have at least one more reader that has delved into the story and gotten some tidbit of enjoyment. So, I dedicate this book to the 'first readers' those that read the first book and keep asking for more. Thanks for the encouragement!

1 / VISITORS

"Comp'ny comin'," declared Ezra. He turned to look at his friend who sat in the chair beside him. They were enjoying their morning coffee, sitting on the porch of their cabin, high in the foothills of the Bitterroot Mountains. The day started with promise, cool clear air, birds high in the surrounding pines singing their morning melodies, blue sky with nary a cloud, and good friends and family round about.

Ezra was Ezra Blackwell, son of the prominent pastor of the Mother Bethel African Methodist Episcopal church of Philadelphia, and lifelong friend of Gabriel Stonecroft. Married to Grey Dove of the Shoshone, and father to their son, Chipmunk, and six-month-old daughter, Squirrel. Ezra was a proven warrior who had earned the name Black Buffalo from an early visit to the Arapaho people when he and Gabriel fought the raiding Ute alongside the Arapaho.

It was in that same battle that Gabriel was given the name Spirit Bear after the pale colored bears of the far north that always fought valiantly.

Gabriel, or Gabe as he was most often called, had taken Cougar Woman, the war leader of the *Tukku-tikka* band of the Shoshone people, as his wife. They had a six-month-old son, Bobcat together and the two families were more of one extended family and lived together in the cabin they built in the Bitterroot foothills, in the narrow valley above the small lakes that would one day be known as Miner Lakes.

Gabe had been busy cleaning his rifle, the unique Ferguson rifle, a breech-loading flintlock he received as a gift from his father's extensive weapons collection. It was a collection that also yielded two double barreled French over/under pistols that rode in their saddle holsters, a pair of Bailes swivel double barreled pistols, one of which had been given to Ezra, and some handcrafted Flemish knives. But Gabe's most often preferred weapon was his Mongol bow, another pick of his father's collection, a unique recurve bow used by the ancient Mongols and in the hands of a skilled archer such as Gabe, had a range that could exceed four hundred yards. He dropped his hand to the big black wolf that lay beside him, running his fingers through the beast's scruff, and spoke to him, "So, Wolf, you're bein' mighty lazy today. You must have recognized our visitors 'fore we did, huh?"

In their extensive travels since leaving Philadelphia a few days ahead of bounty hunters, the two men had become well-known among many different native tribes west of the Mississippi river. They had lived with several, and now were neighbors and friends to a band of Salish led by their chief Plenty Bears and their war leader, Spotted Eagle.

The early part of this summer had been spent taking a young Nez Percé warrior, who had been a captive of the Blackfoot, back to his people beyond the Bitterroots. They were enjoying their time at home in their well-built cabin and the women especially were appreciative of the security for their little ones, who could be heard playing in the cabin while their mothers worked at preparing the mid-day meal.

Gabe stood his rifle against the wall, came to his feet, and walked to the edge of the porch to lean on the post. Ezra had already cocked one hip on the porch rail and was watching the visitors come toward the cabin on the trail through the tall pines. Gabe lifted his hand, palm open and forward, *"Ɂe Ɂa"* he said, the typical greeting *"Ah eh"* he repeated. He had recognized Spotted Eagle and his oldest son, Red Hawk. Two others were with them, but Gabe did not recognize them right off. When Spotted Eagle returned the greeting, Gabe motioned them closer, and took the steps down as they neared.

"It is good to see you Spotted Eagle. What brings

you this way?" asked Gabe as he motioned the visitors to step down.

"We have been scouting for the buffalo, this is not a good year for the buffalo," answered Spotted Eagle.

"How so?" inquired Ezra, joining the men at the foot of the steps.

"When they know a hard winter comes, they do not move as far north but stay in the low flatlands."

"Hello, Spotted Eagle, and Red Hawk! So good to see you!" came a surprised voice from the porch. Gabe turned to see Cougar Woman and Grey Dove, both with little ones on their hips as they leaned against the porch rail.

Red Hawk stepped closer, "Cougar Woman, Grey Dove, it has been too long!"

Cougar looked down at Gabe, "The meal is ready if you are!" giving a motion to include the visitors, "Or would you rather eat on the porch?"

Gabe looked at Eagle, saw the slight nod and answered, "We'll prob'ly eat on the porch."

"Then come inside and dish it up," offered Cougar, turning to go back into the cabin.

With plates and cups full, the men returned to the porch, but Cougar and Dove kept Red Hawk inside, anxious to hear about the other young people of the Salish village. It had been just the past winter when many of the young people had been taken captive by a band of raiding Blackfoot, but Gabe and Cougar had freed many and kept them at the cabin for a few days. And they were pleasant days as the women taught and learned from the young people, all becoming good friends and Red Hawk was one of the leaders of the group.

Gabe asked, "Did you find any buffalo?"

"Yes, but they are much further away than usual at this time of year." He nodded toward the south, "There is a good herd in the valley of the Snake River," then motioned to the east, "another beyond those hills, but that is Blackfoot and Crow country."

"And to the south?" asked Gabe, taking a sip of the hot coffee.

"The Shoshone, but we are friends with the Shoshone. But west of the Shoshone are the Paiute."

Gabe glanced at the expression of Spotted Eagle, "I take it you're not friends with the Paiute?"

"They are diggers, not hunters like we are, but they are not like the Blackfoot," explained Spotted Eagle.

"What do you mean, diggers?" asked Ezra.

"Most of their food comes from the ground. They grow much but dig more."

"You mean like Bitterroot? And Camas?" inquired Gabe.

"Yes."

Gabe glanced at Ezra, both men thinking the Salish also dig for the Bitterroot and Camas and more. Then he looked at Eagle, "Does that mean you are friends with the Paiute?"

Spotted Eagle sighed heavily, glanced at his fellow scout, his long-time friend, Running Wolf who dropped his eyes to his food. Then Eagle said, "We are not enemies."

"So, what will your people do? About the Buffalo, I mean."

"We will go south, but it is four, five days from our village. It will be hard, but we must."

"Want some company?" asked Gabe, looking from Eagle to Running Wolf.

Ezra glanced at Gabe, then at Eagle, anxious for his answer. A buffalo hunt was always an exciting and gratifying time, sometimes dangerous, but always rewarding.

"It would be good to have you with us," answered Eagle, smiling.

Gabe nodded, grinning, then asked, "So, those colts drop yet?" He was referring to three mares in foal by his big black Andalusian stallion, Ebony. It had been part of a wager between the men about the range of the Mongol bow, a weapon never before seen by the Salish and Gabe had compromised with a breeding of Spotted Eagle's mares.

"Yes! And one looks just like your stallion!" declared Eagle, proudly.

Gabe grinned, "The one out of that appaloosa I

traded you out of looks just like I expected, all black but with a spotted rump, just like his mama." He looked at Spotted Eagle, "Has Red Hawk started his training like he wanted?" Gabe knew there had been a bit of a conflict between Spotted Eagle and his son about the boy's thoughts on training and he saw Eagle shake his head slightly.

"He has strange ways, that boy. But I promised him, and he has started. He thinks he can be a friend with the foals. That has never been done by our people, but he has much to learn. That is how it is with the young, they must learn for themselves," groused Eagle, glancing toward the cabin where his son was visiting with the women.

"It is not easy teaching the young," started Gabe, glancing to Ezra and back to Spotted Eagle, "as we are beginning to learn ourselves." He chuckled, knowing there would be much for him to learn about the raising and teaching of children. But there would be lots of time and if God blessed, there would be a house full of young ones between the two couples.

2 / JOURNEY

"Spotted Eagle said it was about four or five days from their village and we're a day closer, so, three or four to get there, couple days huntin', three or four back, maybe more. So, ten days or so," explained Gabe, sitting beside Cougar at the table.

Ezra and Dove were listening closely as well and Dove looked at Ezra, "I think I would stay here, with the children. We have traveled much, and it would be good to stay home," she declared, nodding as if agreeing with herself and with a glance to Cougar.

Gabe looked at his wife, then to Dove and Ezra. As he drank the last of his coffee, he thought a moment, then looked at Cougar, "How 'bout'chu?"

"It would be good for you," nodding to Gabe and Ezra, "to do some hunting alone. But that would mean you would have to dress and skin the animals without our help."

Gabe scrunched his face, "I think we've done that a time or two before, ya reckon?" looking at Ezra.

Ezra chuckled, then looked at Dove, "But don't go gettin' all upset if we don't make it back in the time he says," motioning to Gabe. "When Eagle and his bunch get down there, we might find ourselves in who knows what."

"But if we start out in the mornin', we'll get the jump on 'em and maybe be on our way back by the time they get there!" offered Gabe.

"Well, I'm still a little curious though," responded a grinning Ezra.

"Curious? About what?"

"About whatever it will be or whoever it will be that you find that you just can't keep from helpin' out of some kinda trouble."

The women both laughed, looked at Gabe and reveled in his discombobulated expression, knowing the truth of Ezra's remark. It seemed to be the nature of the man that wherever he went, he always found someone in dire need of help in one way or another and it was not in him to deny anyone that helping hand.

"Now, hold on there. Where we're goin' the only people that'll be there will be the Salish with Spotted Eagle and a few thousand wooly buggers that you're named after! So, how can I get involved in gettin' somebody out of trouble? Huh? Tell me!" proclaimed an exasperated Gabe.

"Not my doin', it's you. You attract trouble like spring flowers attract bees! Only they got sense enough to fly away!" responded Ezra, laughing at his friend.

Cougar leaned over, laying her head on his shoulder, and tucking her hand under his elbow, "That is how you are, my husband and I like you like that!"

Three horses and the mule stood tethered to the hitch rail in front of the cabin. The mule would be carrying the packsaddle and panniers with their trappings, the big grey gelding packhorse would have an empty packsaddle and panniers in anticipation to bringing home considerable meat. Gabe's black Andalusian stallion, Ebony, stood watching curiously as the men gathered their gear and Ezra's long-legged bay gelding stood head down and disinterested.

Once the animals were geared up, the men embraced their wives and stepped beside the horses, slipped their rifles into the scabbards, pistols in the saddle holsters, and checked the rest of their gear. Ezra slid his rifle stock shaped ironwood warclub with the razor-sharp halberd blade into the sheath beneath his saddle fender opposite the Lancaster rifle and although he had a Bailes double barreled swivel pistol that matched Gabe's in his belt, up until recently he had been under gunned. But when the two shared in the battle between the Hudson's Bay renegades and the Northwest Company traders, he gained an additional pistol that now rested in a holster beside the pommel. Gabe's Mongol bow, in its watertight case, hung opposite his rifle under his left leg and saddle fender, the quiver hung from the tie-down behind the cantle. When their weapons were secured, they stepped into the stirrups and swung aboard, bent down and kissed their wives again, then reined around to start down the switch-back trail to the valley below.

When they broke from the trees at the valley floor, a big bull moose lifted his velvet antlers from the water, lake bottom greenery hanging from his jowls, and turned to look at the passersby. Wolf had spotted the moose early on, but he was not interested and continued his scout of the trail ahead. Unconcerned, the big bull dipped his head back into the shallow water to finish his early morning snack. Gabe said, "You better be careful Mr. Moose, if Cougar Woman sees you, you'll be smoking on her racks by sundown!"

Ezra chuckled, "She is kinda partial to moose meat, ain't she?!"

"She is that, but I also remember the first time we met her, we were on our way to the Grand Encampment with the Shoshone and she and her band of scouts joined up with us. We had a little run-in with some Blackfoot, then she and I went after some meat with my bow. She could not believe that I could take down a big elk with one arrow. I think that's when she decided she wanted to spend more time with me!"

"Her? You mean you! That's when you started lookin' at her like a woman instead of the war leader of the Shoshone!"

"Now, what self-respectin' man would want to marry up with a war leader of an Indian tribe? Most folks have no idea that a woman can be a warrior, much less a war leader!" answered Gabe, chuckling. "But you're right, she turned my head that day, she did and I ain't looked the other way since."

"Wouldn't be too healthy if you did," drawled Ezra, giving his friend a sidelong glance as they turned into the rising sun and shielded their eyes with their hands. It was that first glare of the morning sun as it bent its lances of gold over the eastern horizon. The day had shown promise with a cloudless sky and a cool breeze that brushed their right cheeks as it came from the high granite peaks that still held crevices of snow near timberline.

Both men had developed the habit of spending the first moments of every day with their Lord and this morning's time would be in the saddle, but special, nevertheless. They rode silently, each man petitioning his Lord in his own way and words, always with a grateful heart for their lives, families, and surroundings. Gabe had often said, "It's mighty difficult to look about us at this amazing country and not be thankful to God almighty for what He has done." And this morning was no exception. With the rising sun casting a pale pink tint to the timbered mountains, the brightness of the golden orb painting the tips of the peaks with gold, then sliding the glow of daylight down the rugged slopes to the trail before them, with long shadows of tall timber stretched across the deep ravines that divided the mountains. Gabe sucked deep of the clear mountain air and smiled, wonder painting his face as he reveled in the beauty of the Rocky Mountains.

The horses were fresh, and they rode past midday when they turned south from the wide valley of the Big Hole River and into the sparse timber at the edge of another valley that led to the south flats and hopefully the buffalo herds. They stopped at the edge of a spring fed and willow shrouded creek that twisted around the heavy timber and opened into the wide valley. Loosening the girths on the horses and the mule, the men let them drink at the creek and picketed them on the nearby grass. With some juniper at the edge of a slight knob that offered some shade, Gabe fetched some smoked meat from the pannier, and they sat in the shade to stretch out and relax while they munched on the usual fare of the trail.

Wolf stretched out beside Gabe, his head between his paws as he enjoyed the man stroking his fur behind his ears. But Wolf's head came up, ears pricked forward, and he rose to all fours. Gabe and Ezra looked in the direction where Wolf stared, and Ezra said, "The horses are lookin' too."

At the far edge of the trees, beyond the creek and the grass where the horses were tethered, movement showed at the tree line. A big grey wolf trotted from the shadows, sided by a dingy white and slightly smaller wolf. Two more came close behind, but in between the four adults, a half-dozen fur ball pups trotted playfully, trying to keep up with the leaders. The big grey male stopped and looked directly at the horses, then saw the men and the black wolf at the trees. He lifted his head and stood tall and proud, glaring at the intruders to his territory.

Gabe rose slowly and with Wolf at his side, walked to the horses, keeping his eyes on the wolf pack. As he watched, two more came from the trees, both grey, and all had stopped to look their direction. Gabe slowly reached for his rifle, slipping it unhurriedly from the scabbard as Ebony stood stock still, head high, ears pricked, as he looked at the wolves. Although the big stallion and the black wolf beside Gabe were friends, the big horse knew danger when he saw it and a hungry pack of wolves could be trouble.

Gabe stepped back from his horse, glanced at Wolf, and saw his hackles were raised and he stood in a threatening and challenging posture. Gabe could easily tell that Wolf had the size over the pack leader, but he would not move without Gabe's word. Gabe glanced to double-check the load on his rifle, eared back the hammer and lifted the Ferguson rifle to his shoulder. Although the adult wolves had not moved, the pups had no idea what was happening and playfully ran and tumbled over one another, one bumping into the pack leader and received a quick snap and growl to send him on his way. But it was that break in his stance that changed the mood and the tone of the confrontation, and the leader glanced at the rest of the pack, then with another glaring look across the narrow valley at the big black wolf that stood by the man, he turned away and trotted off, the others trailing close behind.

"That was interesting," said Ezra, standing beside his horse with his rifle in hand. Gabe had not seen him come near but was not surprised at his friend who always sided him, no matter the trouble or challenge.

"Yeah, wasn't it though. I didn't think they'd do anything, not with the pups along, but, you never can tell," stated Gabe. "Let's give 'em a little time to get wherever they're goin' then we'll hit the trail again. 'sides, I left my jerky back there," nodding to the trees and the welcoming shade.

3 / PLAINS

They appeared to be a mis-matched pair. Gabe stood right at six feet, broad shouldered, dirty blonde hair that hung almost to his shoulders, and narrow hipped, appearing lean, he was deceptively strong. Deep blue piercing eyes under a broad forehead, high cheekbones and square jawed, he had the looks that turned the eyes of most women. From his time in the university, to his ramblings in the wilderness, his confidence came from training at the hands of both the heavyweight boxing champion Daniel Mendoza and his successor, Gentleman John Jackson. With additional instruction in a specialized discipline of Jujutsu and first-hand experience against keelboaters, Indians, renegades, runaway slaves, and bounty hunters, he had repeatedly proven his worth in any combat. And now, outfitted in beaded and fringed buckskins, he revealed nothing of his past.

Ezra was almost his opposite. Shorter and built like a whiskey barrel with a deep chest, bulging muscles across his chest, shoulders, and upper arms. With legs like stumps, when he took a broad stance with his war club, he was immovable and deadly. His dark brown complexion was reminiscent of his father, a former slave and now a pastor, and his Black Irish mother who hailed from Druid and Celtic stock, from whom he gained his precognitive abilities and more. The only similarities between the two were their manner of dress, Ezra was also arrayed in buckskins lovingly fashioned and beaded by his Shoshone wife, Grey Dove.

The two men had been friends since boyhood when they roamed the forests of Pennsylvania together, using every moment to sharpen their woodsmen skills and their love of the wilderness. When Gabe killed a ne'er do well rich man's son in a duel, the two had left the east with bounty hunters on their tail. The rich and influential father of the insulting dead man had placed a sizable, though illegal, bounty on Gabriel's head. To avoid dishonoring his father, Gabe left and Ezra would not be left behind, as the two men sought to fulfill a lifelong dream to explore the wilderness known as French Louisiana.

Never prone to waste daylight, they were on the south-bound trail when the rising sun chased the

retreating darkness beyond the western mountains.
Wolf trotted before them, scouting their trail and
looking for his breakfast. The big beast, well over
a hundred fifty pounds, was almost too tall to walk
under Ebony's belly, but the two had been best friends
since Wolf was found as a pup in the cavern behind
their first cabin. The sun stood over their left shoulder
when Wolf stopped, dropped his head, and snarled,
showing his teeth as he looked to their left toward the
tree line as the valley narrowed.

Gabe saw the wolf pack, sidling along the low
slope, moving in and out of the trees, but always
watching the men and horses. There were six big
wolves, and the pups still traveled with them. Gabe
noticed the stance of Wolf as he glowered and snarled
at the pack. He lifted his head high, watching the pack
and broadened the stance of his front feet, looking as
if he would pounce from the trail across the narrow
valley to the wolves that were at least a hundred yards
distant. When the pack moved into the thicker timber
and out of sight, Wolf visibly relaxed and looked over
his shoulder to Gabe, who nodded, giving the wolf
permission to continue his scout on the trail.

Gabe glanced at Ezra, "Don't like seein' that pack
shadowin' us. Either they have plans on movin' in on
us, or maybe meetin' with Wolf in a fight."

"One thing for certain," drawled Ezra, "you cain't
never tell about them wolves. When they're in a pack

like that, they do whatever they please. Remember when we seen that pack take down that big bull buffalo last winter?"

"Yeah. They're a lot like humans, whenever they're in a pack, they'll do what they daren't do when they're alone!"

They had ridden just over a mile when Wolf stopped again, hackles up, and watching the wolf pack come from the trees and cross the valley and the trail to move to the west side and the black timber. A quick glance showed the hills on the east were barren, with no more than scattered bunch grass, a variety of cacti and a lot of nothing but rolling hills. The west edge was thick with timber, spruce, fir, pine and more. And while the hills on the east were low and rolling, those foothills of the mountains on the west were knobs, buttes, and ridges, all with thick timber. Just the kind of country the wolves preferred to hide in when they stalked their prey.

By mid-day, they could see the mouth of the valley which had bent easterly, but they chose to rest up beside the creek that had pushed to the west edge and lay in the shadow of the tall pines. The hills on both sides pushed into the valley, narrowing the green stretch that rode the side of the little creek. The timber on the west edge thinned out, showing sparse patches that were littered with juniper, cedar, and piñon. Early afternoon they broke from the valley into the barren flats. The wide flood plain was littered with a myriad of streams, most showing boggy land about as the streams meandered, joining, and splitting across the flats. Cattail bogs were interspersed with small pools decorated with lazy lily pads showing big white blossoms. Scraggly alder and willow clung tenaciously to the low banks, and the wide plain was bordered by knobby and barren hills on the south, rolling desolate hills on the north, and in the distance and downstream to the east, a lone butte that resembled a giant ant hill glared across the flat to a lower but colorful round-top.

Everywhere they looked, the tan and brown shades melded together to give a dusty panorama. The men reined up and looked round about, studying the terrain. Gabe nodded to their right, "Those mountains look a long way off!" He nodded to the long line of granite peaks, a few showing white at the tops that marched like uniformed soldiers into the barren flats to the south.

"Yeah, but, according to Spotted Eagle, that flat land yonder," pointing to the south, "is where we'll find the buffalo!" countered Ezra.

Gabe stood in his stirrups and turned to look behind them. "Those wolves are stayin' in the timber. I can see that curly pack leader standing on that knob. I think he was frettin' 'bout Wolf here maybe goin' after his lady friends."

"Well, Wolf's love life might be important to him, but I'm more concerned about some fresh buffalo steaks!"

They turned south, crossing a trio of long, dry, ridges that separated two conjoining rivers. Once over the ridges, they lined out on a gunsight cut in the distant mountains and traversed the rolling hills, bound for that cut. It was coming on dusk when they neared the notch, and Gabe took the high land for a promontory to overlook the valley beyond. It was ever his habit to know where he was going, even if it was country that had never known his footprint and did so by often using his brass telescope to judge the lay of the land and the possible dangers it might hold.

They made camp in a horseshoe shaped hollow that offered cover, ample firewood, and tall trees for a windbreak. Grass was abundant in the evening shadowed clearing, and Gabe made a quick foray to the hilltop for his looksee. With Wolf at his side, he found a flat limestone rock and took his seat. As he stretched out his scope, he looked at the valley below. As near as he could judge, it was about ten miles across the flat before the foothills of a series of tall mountains framed the western edge of the long valley. Stretching as far as he could see to the southeast, the valley, though at first glance appeared barren, showed tall grasses, mostly browned by the hot sun, waving in the evening breeze. A mixture of bunch grass, Indian grass, and foxtail, littered the valley, all graze that buffalo craved.

He moved his scope along the tip of the peaks, remembering that Spotted Eagle told them the flat-lands beyond the ridges of the mountains is where the buffalo would be found. It was beyond his view in the dim light of dusk for him to see the promised bounty, but he grinned as he scanned the broad vis-ta. This was big land and even in the midst of what appeared to be barren country, green showed the chosen course of the many streams that were fed by snow melt and deep springs. Greenery that gave life to the abundance of wild game and the many different people that claimed this country as their own. This was land that was hunted by the Shoshone, Bannock, and Paiute, and of course the more distant tribes like the Salish, Crow and Blackfoot.

When Gabe walked back into camp, Ezra already had a fire going and a pot of coffee dancing on a flat rock at the side. He glanced up as Gabe came near, "See anything?"

"Some mighty big country. That valley yonder," pointing with his chin, "is 'bout ten miles wide and goes further'n I can see. That long line of peaks marches alongside it clear down yonder."

"How far ya reckon?" asked Ezra, piercing some smoked meat on a green willow to hang over the flames.

"Couple days, at least!"

Ezra frowned, "I thought Spotted Eagle said it was only four, five days from their village!?"

"He did, but he coulda seen buffalo just about anywhere. There might even be some in the lower end of this valley or could be they lined out in the broad plains beyond."

Their conversation was interrupted when Wolf jumped to his feet and went to the edge of the clearing and the long howl of a lone wolf, somewhere in the first dark of night, drifted over the tree tops. Wolf lifted his head and answered the call, letting his mournful howl carry across the flats and end with the repeated short howls as his chest bounced with the effort. Silence blanketed the camp. The horses had lifted their heads but did not move. Gabe sat still, steam rising from the cup in his hands, as he glanced at Ezra, now on one knee beside the fire and looking toward Wolf. Another distant howl sounded, and Wolf answered. He looked over his shoulder at the men, and at the slight nod from Gabe, Wolf disappeared into the night.

4 / FLATS

Gabe was not surprised, but he was pleased that the first image that focused in his sleep filled eyes was the deep black fur on the back of Wolf as he lay beside the blankets. Gabe reached out and ran his fingers through the thick scruff of his long-time friend and companion, letting him know he was missed and welcomed back. He had been gone all night, not an unusual behavior for the wolf and he had always returned, but this time was different. Gabe sniffed the air and frowned, there was a distinct odor, a bitter but not overpowering stench and it seemed to be in the wolf's fur. After a quick survey of the camp, Gabe threw off his blankets and sat up, looking around for any strange creatures, maybe a female pack member that followed Wolf into the camp. But he saw nothing, the horses were standing hipshot and unalarmed and Gabe slowly rose to his feet, slipping his pistol in his belt and reaching for his rifle.

A quick glance at the sleeping form in the other blankets showed Ezra was still enjoying his rest. The dim early light of morning was too faint to pierce the pines and Gabe walked around the clearing, looking into the deep shadow of the woods, seeing nothing amiss. Returning to the grey ashes of the previous nights' cookfire, he splintered off some kindling from a chunk of wood and pushed the coals around until he found a handful of hot ones. With the kindling pyramided over the coals, he blew softly until a small flame rose, then he carefully lay on some larger sticks and more until the fire was flaring nicely. He stood to brush off the ashes that blew back on his shoulders and face, then picked up the coffee pot and started for the creek. He paused, turned back, and slipped his bow from its case, sat down and strung it, then with quiver dangling from his belt and bow in one hand, coffee pot in the other, he left the clearing.

It was just a trickle of a run-off creek, draining the higher mountains from the last of the lingering snow, but it was cold, clear, and would make mighty good coffee. That's what Gabe was thinking about when he stopped dead in his tracks as he saw Wolf drop to his belly. At the edge of the creek, two young mule deer bucks had just dropped their heads to the water for a drink. Gabe went to one knee, sat down the coffeepot, and nocked an arrow. He took a deep

breath, started his draw, and waited until the bucks
lifted their heads. It would be an off-shoulder shot,
but he was confident he could make it. He slowly
brought it to full draw, then sighted just behind the
front shoulder and released the arrow. It was no more
than fifty yards, and the arrow flew true, burying itself into the ribs behind the right front shoulder and
traveling at an angle to push through the left flank.
The impact pushed the buck back a step, alarmed the
second animal that jumped almost straight up and
was bounding off as the first one fell to the ground.
Gabe waited a moment, nocking another arrow as he
stood, then walked toward the creek and the downed
buck, coffeepot in hand.

He made short work of field-dressing the deer.
With a large piece of hide, he cut out the backstraps,
tenderloins, rump, and round steaks. He left the gut
pile and the trimmings for the scavengers, knowing all of God's creatures must eat and they would
soon be swarming over the morning's feast. There
would be coyotes, badgers, magpies, ravens, turkey
buzzards, and many others that would share in the
bounty, nothing would be wasted. Of course, Wolf
got his share with almost every cut of the blade and
he was well satisfied as he walked back to camp at
Gabe's side.

Ezra rolled from the blankets when the smell of
fresh coffee stirred him to wakefulness. He sat up,

stretched, and saw the fresh strips of backstrap sizzling over the low flames and said, "You been at it kinda early this mornin' ain'tchu?"

"No, you're just a little slow gettin' around," answered Gabe. "It's a beautiful mornin' and we've still got a ways to go, so roll 'em out, sleepyhead!"

Ezra frowned, wrinkling his nose, and glanced around the camp, "Did we have a visitor last night or sumpin'?"

"You mean that smell?"

Ezra nodded his head as he stood and stretched again, "Ummhmm," he groaned.

"Wolf brought that back with him."

"If I didn't know better, I'd say he been rollin' with the bears!" drawled Ezra, reaching for the lid of the coffeepot. He flipped it back and dropped the handful of coffee grounds he scraped up from the rock after he pounded them into dust.

"I thought it might be from his amorous escapades after that invitation he got last night."

"Could be, but . . ." answered Ezra, turning to go into the trees for his morning routine.

After the coffeepot did its dance for several minutes, Gabe slid it back and poured some of the reserved cold water in to settle the grounds, then poured himself a cup. He was sitting back against the downed log when Ezra returned and watched as his friend poured a cup.

Ezra glanced at Gabe, "Reckon we'll hit the flats today?"

"Oh, the valley down yonder is pretty much like the flats, but dunno if we'll find any big woolies, although it would be good country for 'em. But by the end of the day, we'll be within sight of the plains that Spotted Eagle spoke about."

"Well, looks to me like those steaks are ready, so," as he reached out to pick a willow with a dangling strip of broiled meat, "I'll just force myself to partake!" He leaned back and tore a chunk from the bigger strip with his teeth, grinning as the juices dripped through his whiskers. Neither man was fond of heavy whiskers and now showed about a week's worth of growth, the stubble scratchy on their collars, but they would wait until they were nearer deep water before taking a dip and washing off the dirt and whiskers of the trail.

The long valley was bounded on both sides by a long line of peaks, stretching back to the west to the taller Bitterroots and east to the plains of the flatlands that rode the banks of the Snake River. They had been traveling all day, with only a short break at noon, and were now looking for a place to stop for the night. This valley was like others that paralleled it and stretched east with skeletal fingers from the bones of the Bitterroots. The only water was the runoff from the higher mountains and usually flowed most of the summer, for the high mountains held to the deep snows packed into the crevasses until the long hot summer sun chased the snowmelt into the lower reaches. But they seldom released the last of the glaciers until the sun had done its worst, baking the limestone and granite high above timberline. The bottom of the valley was a mish mash of alluvial plains that stretched out like grandma's aprons to spread their wealth of silt and sand across the valley floor. The rich black topsoil, washed down from on high, sprouted green with grasses and flowers, decorating the broad expanse with color.

As the two men rode alongside the gurgling creek, they saw abundant sign of game. Moose, elk, deer, mountain sheep, grizzly bear, black bear, and many wolves, coyotes, and smaller game. But there was no sign of man. Gabe looked at Ezra, "You notice there's not been any sign of man or horses, even mustangs?"

"Yeah, but as you know, that doesn't mean there hasn't been any, just that there hasn't been any around here recently!"

"That suits me," responded Gabe, twisting around in his saddle to look at the lowering sun as it lay cradled on the western peaks. The creek they sided, pushed against the steep rocky slopes on the north edge of the valley, forcing the men to cross the creek and follow the meandering brook a short distance downstream where it bent into the valley.

But Gabe saw a deep cut in the steep rocky buttes on the north and pointed with his chin, "Let's make camp on that side, there at the bend with the thicker trees. I think I'd like to shinny up that mountain yonder to take a looksee."

Ezra looked at the steep rocky slopes and asked, "You're gonna climb that?"

Gabe chuckled, "Not that!" nodding to the steep talus slope. "I figger I can go up that ravine yonder, maybe find an easier way up the back side. If I can't, I'll do sumpin' else!" The only thing Gabe was more consistent at than his evening lookabouts, was his prayer time in the morning with his Lord.

Ezra nodded his agreement and the men pushed across the shallow ripples to break into the thickets on the north bank. Gabe dropped the lead to his pack-horse, motioned to Wolf, and started for the ravine. There had been many times that Gabe's reconnoiters had saved their skins and Ezra would not begrudge his friend his routine. Besides, he was anxious to get some more of those backstrap steaks broiling and some coffee perking.

He wasted little time stripping the pack horses and his bay, stacking the gear and giving the animals their well-deserved rubdowns. They drank deep of the cold water and were soon happily grazing on the tall grasses. Ezra got the fire going, keeping it beneath the thick cover of the heavy branches of the cottonwoods, and soon had steaks broiling. They had dug some camas bulbs when they stopped for the midday break and now he buried them in the coals. With the coffee perking and the pot dancing, he leaned back and took in the scenery. The western sky was blazing a brilliant mix of gold and orange, the colors bouncing off the peaks and turning the valley into a muted shade of gold. It was Ezra's favorite time of the day and he leaned back, fingers locked behind his head, legs stretched out and crossed at the ankles and savored the moment as God showed off his splendor.

5 / SIGN

"There's somethin' wrong!" said Ezra. It was written all over Gabe's face, the face of his long-time friend that he could read as if it were written in bold print across his forehead. These two were close, they were wilderness brothers, as different as they were alike and knew each other better than themselves. Ezra, with his added trait of precognition, not only knew his friend, he knew what was bothering him. "It's death, all over the valley," he spoke softly, sitting erect, his eyes closed to slits, "and recent, today."

Gabe nodded, dropped to the log, and stared at the flames, something he would not normally do, knowing the glare of the fire would ruin his night vision. But what he had seen was painted into his mind with the indelible ink of cruel devastation. "Looks like a whole village, probably comin' to hunt. Just tipis and brush huts, nothing permanent. Couldn't tell much from this distance, but the buzzards were circlin'."

"How far?"

"Four, five miles." He lifted his eyes to the sky; the fading light was but a remnant of the golden sunset.

Ezra voiced what he knew Gabe was thinking, "And just a bit ago, I was baskin' in the beauty of a blazing sunset, thinkin' everything was right with the world."

"Yeah."

"Think we oughta go see?" asked Ezra.

"Wouldn't do no good. Moon's nothin' but a sliver, clouds have moved in, couldn't see much to do anything." He tossed a stick into the fire, sparks stair-stepped into the blackness overhead. "We'll go in the mornin'."

After they ate, Ezra set about building some smoke racks from an armful of willows he gathered while he was waiting for Gabe to return. He glanced at his friend, "You know, you could be cuttin' up the rest of that deer meat so we could smoke it. It ain't gonna last another day less'n we do!"

Gabe grinned, "Alright, alright. You're soundin' like an old squaw, naggin' like that!" But he rose and went to the large cuts of meat that lay on the spread open hide and began cutting it into long thin strips. As soon as Ezra had finished erecting the smoke rack, he set it astraddle of the remains of the cookfire and began hanging the strips. Gabe fetched some alder from the edge of the creek, laying it across the coals to start smoking.

When the rack was decorated with the many strips, Gabe sat back on the log, reached for the coffeepot and poured himself a cup. He glanced around the camp, "You seen Wolf?"

"Uhuh, not since 'fore we ate," answered Ezra, pouring himself a cupful of java.

"Wonder if he's gone lookin' for his lady friend," surmised Gabe, sipping on his coffee.

"Prob'ly. But he'll be back."

"Yeah, but if he stinks like he did the last time, I'm gonna throw him in the creek!"

It was a cold nose on his exposed wrist that brought Gabe awake. With one eye open, he saw the familiar figure of Wolf, stretched out, lying on his side, his nose by Gabe's wrist. The pale light showed little, but the unmistakable form of the big wolf was obvious. And as Gabe had developed the practice of looking around the camp without moving anything but his eyes, he made a quick survey, saw nothing amiss, and slowly rose from his blankets. His feet had been toward the fire and as he stretched and yawned, something was not right. Gabe frowned, looking at the mangled smoke rack, devoid of any meat, broken and smashed, it lay as a tangle of twigs beside the grey ashes of the fire.

Gabe made a quick look around, searching for

any varmint that might have caused the damage, looked down at a snoozing Wolf, then rose to his feet. He slipped his pistol into his belt, the knife in the scabbard at his back and the tomahawk opposite the pistol. Reaching for his rifle, he slowly stood, searching for even the tiniest of four-legged varmints that would have absconded with all the smoked meat and destroyed the rack. But there was no sound, no movement. Even the night sounds were missing, no cicadas, no nighthawks, nothing. Gabe frowned and walked closer to the mangled rack, dropped to one knee to examine the destruction, and was surprised to see a jumble of tracks, and not what he expected. Bear tracks.

"How did this happen?" he asked the darkness. Some of the tracks were within inches of the end of his blankets and had passed between his feet and the fire. He looked at Wolf, "Where were you?"

He lifted his eyes to the slowly greying morning sky, treetops silhouetted against the night shroud that now faded from deep black to dark grey. Gabe calculated, "The sun'll rise in about a half-hour," then dropped his eyes to the tracks in the soft soil beside the rack. He looked as best he could in the dim light but was able to determine the tracks were those of a black bear, claw tips of forepaws were close to the toes and toes were in an arced line. *A grizz has bigger paws, longer claws,* he thought. *And this'n ain't very big either. Prob'ly a yearlin', no more'n two years old, prob'ly younger. But, why come into camp with all the smell of man and horse?* He shook his head as he stood, then chose to make a circuit of the camp, to see where the bear went when he left. He sniffed the air, got a whiff much like the day before, then a slow grin started to split his face. He looked down at Wolf, "Were you runnin' with the bears the last two nights? It sure smells the same!" he had spoken softly, but Ezra stirred, nevertheless.

Ezra scrunched his nose, turned with a frown and glared at Gabe, "So, it was Wolf, wasn't it. What'd he do, get him a stinker of a girlfriend?" Ezra was still seated, the blankets covering his legs, as he looked around the camp. He saw the destroyed rack and looked up at Gabe, "What did that?"

"A bear! Looks like a yearlin' black bear. But what gets me is where was he," pointing with his chin to Wolf, "when this was happenin'."

It was just a short while till they were back on the trail, pack horse and mule following, neither with leads. The big grey had buddied up with Ebony and followed him and the mule had taken a liking to Ezra and stayed right behind him. Gabe shaded his eyes from the glare of the rising sun, looking to the sky for the circling buzzards, but the sky was empty. "Reckon them buzzards are already feastin' on the carcasses of whatever's down."

"You were too far away to see much detail, could it have been dead horses or sumpin'?" asked Ezra.

"Mebbe, but there was nothing moving among the shelters. If there had been people, live people, I coulda seen some movement. But there was nothing. Just the turkey buzzards circling."

"Course, they do that when they *suspect* somethin's gonna die, even before there is anything dead. You don't suppose it's some kinda plague or somethin', do ya?"

They both knew of tribes that had been infected with white man's disease, minor illnesses for white people, but for the natives that had no immunity, they were deadly. After infected traders had visited the camps, measles, mumps, smallpox and more had swept through native villages and killed hundreds. Some unscrupulous traders had taken blankets and goods from infected villages and traded them to other natives, spreading the plague further.

As they neared the village, they reined up and Gabe reached back for his looking glass. He stretched it out and focused it on the sight before them, sighed heavily and handed the scope to Ezra. Both men were shaking their heads, having seen the assortment of carrion eaters busy at their feast. Some bodies had several scavengers fighting over them, but others had a single badger, bobcat, or eagle taking their fill. It was as if some message went out on the bloody board of the forest summoning every hungry predator to a feast.

As they came closer, Ezra said, "This weren't no plague! If it was, it was the plague of greed and gore!" He pointed with his chin, "See there," directing their attention to the nearest body, "they made a pincushion outta him. He musta run a ways and fell to break off them arrows, otherwise they'da taken 'em outta him."

As they rode through the temporary village of pine bough lean-tos, blanket covered brush huts, a few hide tipis, and scattered bodies, it was a gruesome sight. Every single body, regardless of sex or age, had been mutilated, scalped, and stripped of anything of use to the raiders. Genitals had been cut off, bodies sliced, fingers and feet removed, all because of vendettas based on superstition. There were bodies of youngsters, no more than toddlers, babies in cradleboards, old people with white hair dipped in blood. As they rode through, carrion eaters scattered, some hissing and growling before they surrendered their feast, some ignoring the riders and continuing uninterrupted.

The men reined up, their backs to the massacre, looked at one another and Gabe pointed to the west edge of the village, "There's a deep ravine yonder, we could drag the bodies there, cave it in over 'em and there's some big rocks we can roll down there too."

Ezra looked at his friend, "You know what you're sayin'? There's what, sixty, seventy bodies there? That'd take us most of a day!"

"Yeah, prob'ly. But we can't leave 'em there. They're already stinkin' somethin' fierce and won't no self-respecting buffalo gonna come within smellin' distance! 'Sides, it's the right thing to do."

Ezra shook his head, "We've left dead unburied before."

"Yeah, but they were usually tryin' to kill us and didn't deserve no better. But these folks, those women and kids, they didn't deserve this."

"Alright. Let's get busy with the buryin'."

They stripped the packs off the grey and the mule, loosened the girths on their horses, and picketed them near the grass and started into the village, leading the pack animals. Gabe stripped a hide from a tipi, used a braided rawhide rope and fashioned a travois from the poles from the hide lodge. Ezra used the mule to drag the bodies near, then the travois was used to take the load of bodies to the ravine. It was approaching mid-day when the men were finished with their grisly task and stood at the edge of the ravine and started pushing the bank off to cover the stack of bodies. They had counted seventy-eight bodies and saw no sign of any others. But the sign left behind by the raiders was obvious and they pieced together what had happened.

"Prob'ly started 'bout sun-up, and there was so many of 'em, the people didn't have much of a chance. What'chu figger, fifty, sixty warriors?" started Ezra, looking at his friend.

"I'd say 'bout that, maybe more, but there's something a little puzzling. There were youngsters, you know, little ones 'bout eight or ten and younger. And there were adults, warriors, women, old people. But there weren't very many young people, you know, from 'bout twelve up to twenty."

Ezra frowned, "You don't s'pose. . ."

"That's exactly what I'm sayin'. Not only did the raiders take all the horses, and there were plenty of 'em, but they took the young people too."

"Who do you think they were, the raiders I mean?"

"Dunno. I'm not too sure who the people of the village were. I'm thinkin' maybe Paiute, but not sure."

The men were waist deep in the backwater pool of the creek, scrubbing off the blood and stench of death as they talked. Their rifles were close at hand and a clean set of buckskins were laid out beside them. Ezra had lathered up his thick head of hair and covered his face and neck with the white soapy lather from the lye soap, when Gabe said, "Uh, we got comp'ny!" He spoke softly, but the announcement froze Ezra in place, but he ducked under water and came up spitting, and looked to see three people standing just beyond the rifles and buckskins, staring at the men in the water.

6 / LEARNING

An old man, a young boy of about ten summers, and a girl of about five of six summers, stood before them. The old man with long grey streaked hair that hung below his shoulders, was arrayed in buckskin leggings, a breechcloth, and a buckskin shirt that showed a thin line of beading across the yoke. The sleeves were fringed, but ragged, and the leggings also showed ragged fringe. Tattered and worn moccasins adorned his feet. The youngsters were in leggings and a dress, but the boy was bare chested. All had stoic expressions that showed grief, fear, and anger. The old man's hand rested on the boy's shoulder and he began to speak in both sign and the language of his people.

"I am Lone Bear of the Numa people, some call us Paiute. We are of the Koa'aga'itöka," he had signed *Salmon Caught in Traps Eaters.* "We saw what you did with our people and we are grateful."

Gabe signed to the man, "I am Spirit Bear, and this is Black Buffalo. Our wives are Shoshone, and we are friends with most natives, but we have not known any Paiute." He paused, motioned for them to move back and turn around so they could get out of the water and when they stepped behind some brush, Gabe and Ezra came from the water, drying themselves off with a blanket and quickly dressed. When they were finished, he called out to the visitors to come back.

Gabe continued signing, "Who did this to your people?"

"Liksiyu! Some call them *Waiilatpus*, people of the Rye Grass!" he glowered as he spoke and signed. "They are long-time enemies of our people and the Shoshone and Bannock people. They raid for horses and captives. They are a vile people!"

"Did they take captives from your village?" asked Ezra.

"Yes, but I do not know how many."

"Are you hungry?" asked Gabe, looking at the empty eyes of the little girl.

When the girl's eyes widened, and the boy nodded, Gabe went to the parfleche on the mule and dug out some smoked meat and pemmican for the three. It was eagerly received, and quickly consumed. Although they had been without food for just over a day, to a youngster even a few hours without eating can seem like an eternity.

They chose to move a little ways from the site of the village and made camp beside the stream. Ezra glanced at Gabe as they stripped the horses of the gear, "You reckon the Salish will be along soon?"

"Prob'ly. But I been thinkin' about 'em. If they come the same route we took, they'll be alright, but if Spotted Eagle takes them another route and they run into them *Waiilatpus*, there might be trouble."

"Isn't this the way he told us?"

"Yeah, but, we weren't travelin' with women and kids and travois and such. There might be an easier but longer way for them."

"What're we gonna do 'bout them?" asked Ezra, nodding toward the three that were gathering wood for a cookfire.

"Dunno. I'm sure they'd like to get back to their people, wherever that might be, but without horses and such, the youngsters couldn't do it, and neither could that old man."

Ezra chuckled, "So, does this mean a journey into the Paiute country? And what about our womenfolk? We gonna go get them first?"

Gabe shook his head, "Now, let's not go getting the cart before the horse, we might just get 'em some horses and send 'em on their way!"

Ezra feigned looking around, "Don't see no spare horses anywhere, you?"

"Spotted Eagle knows where we'll be, so I reckon

we can wait till they get here before we make any decision 'bout those," pointing with his chin to the three that were stacking firewood beside their chosen spot for the cookfire.

As the men sat with their coffee, they listened as Lone Bear told of the attack by the *Waiilatpus*. As they listened, Gabe and Ezra were beginning to understand some of the words spoken by the old man, the tongue of the Paiute was similar to the Shoshone and with the sign, the words flowed easily. The attack had come at first light and the Paiute were taken completely by surprise, with their warriors intent on hunting buffalo, their thoughts were not on defending against attack. The *Waiilatpus* were known as skilled and fierce warriors, dealing death with lances, arrows, and war clubs, they rode through the village, turned, and dealt death with a vengeance.

"They fought with purpose, a well-planned attack. They must have scouted the village the night before. When they came back through, was when they caught up their captives, lifting them to the backs of the horses, belly down across the withers, and ran off quickly! There were several that rode back through, killing those that still lived. We were there," he pointed to a bluff west of the village, "in the draw beside the bluff, when the attack came." He nodded to the boy, "Antelope wanted to go back and fight, but I would not let him. He had to stay to protect Minnow," nodding to the girl. "We stayed in the trees, there, until morning came. We had gone to find what we could, but there was little left of use. Then we saw you coming and went back to the trees. We were there when you buried the people."

"Their family?" asked Ezra, nodding to the children.

The man just dropped his eyes and shook his head, the children watching.

Gabe nodded to the old man, "I see you have a bow and arrows. Would you join me in a hunt? We will need meat and I thought about going upstream into the valley, maybe find some deer."

"That would be good," replied the old man, he glanced at the boy. "We should bring Antelope with us. He must learn."

Gabe glanced at the boy, saw the start of a grin tug at the corners of his mouth, then looked back to Lone Bear, "That would be good." Gabe had noticed the boy also had a bow and quiver of arrows, although the rangy youth might be good with rabbits and such, to take a deer requires stealth, skill, and enough of a bow to bury the arrow deep, and he doubted the boy's ability with the small bow he had in the quiver. But it was always good for the young to learn from the old, no matter the lesson.

It was mid-afternoon when the three hunters left the camp. Ezra had been coerced into gathering some willow withes to make a smoke rack, and since that was usually the purview of women, it was only natural that Minnow would stay with him. Although there was some grumbling in the process, howbeit not by Minnow for she was fascinated by the black man. The girl had already befriended Wolf and Gabe suggested he stay behind to keep a watch on the girl.

They had traveled just over two hundred yards from camp, when Gabe motioned them to stop and drop into the tall grass. He pointed to the edge of the butte that ended abruptly in the grass, and they saw several deer walking through the deep meadow. The small entourage was pushed by a sizeable buck with antlers still developing and with rags of velvet still hanging. The grass was more than belly deep and the movement told of some fawns running beside their mothers. As they watched, Gabe discerned there were two does, both with fawns, and a third one without a fawn by her side. A young fork-horned buck walked ahead of the big one, staying close behind the solitary doe, their big ears twitching to pick up any sound of danger.

The deer were well over a hundred yards away, and Gabe looked at Antelope, asked with both word and sign, "Which one should we take?"

The boy frowned, lifted up to look at the deer again, then looked to Gabe, also using sign and word, "The small buck."

"Good choice. We can take that one or the single

doe. We only need one." He glanced at Lone Bear, "Should he take the first shot?"

Lone Bear frowned, then looked from Antelope to Gabe and nodded, a slow smile splitting his face. "My grandson will be a good hunter." That was the first time he had referred to the boy as his grandson, which made it easy to understand why the old man had been with the children in the woods. Gabe grinned and nodded, then motioned for them to continue.

They dropped into a crouch as they worked their way closer to the deer, now at the bank of the creek and between clusters of willows. The creek made a sharp horseshoe bend and the cutback, with heavy alder and willows, gave the hunters cover as they drew closer. Gabe motioned for Lone Bear to instruct the boy and to let him get closer and take the first shot. Gabe motioned to his own bow, signing that he would be a back-up. The old man nodded and motioned the boy close. Gabe watched as whispers were exchanged, motions made, and the man rocking back on his heels to let the boy past. As the boy moved, Gabe also moved, but he was in the deep grass and the boy nearer the brush. The boy had already nocked his arrow and slowly rose as he stepped around the brush. In one smooth motion, he brought his bow to full draw and let the arrow fly.

The deer jumped as if they were connected, the young buck the first to move, jumping almost straight

into the air and coming down facing away from the
creek. The big buck turned so quick, he was almost
lying flat on the ground and he sprang away, into the
tall grass, bounding toward the foothills. The young
buck was also bounding, but the feathered fletching
of the arrow waved at his shoulder like a flag. The
does and fawns disappeared in the tall grass. Gabe
allowed the young buck two jumps, then brought his
arrow to full draw, followed the bouncing buck, and
released the feathered shaft. It whispered through the
tops of the grass, found its mark and buried itself deep
in the lower chest of the buck, bearing the animal to
the ground. When Gabe let his arrow fly, the buck
was about sixty yards away, and the arrow sailed true.

Lone Bear had watched the deer bound away,
glanced at Gabe and saw he was readying a shot
and when Lone Bear looked back at the deer, he
thought they were too far away. But the whisper of
the arrow caught his attention and he saw the arrow
impale the buck and drive it to the ground. The old
man froze in place, watching the grass where the
deer fell, waiting for it to rise and take to the hills,
but it did not move. He looked back at Gabe, then
to the boy, and shook his head.

"Grandfather! Did you see what that man did? I
have never seen an arrow fly so far and kill a deer!"
he glanced at the grasses again, then added, "Have
you, Grandfather?"

Lone Bear shook his head, "It is a wonder. I have not seen that done before, no."

Gabe was pushing through the grass, motioned for the others to follow and was soon at the side of the downed buck. A quick glance showed the boy's arrow had struck the deer in the shoulder, found solid purchase in the deep muscle, but was not a killing shot. Gabe's arrow was buried to the fletching in the lower chest just behind the front shoulder and had probably struck the heart, killing the animal almost instantly.

"Look at that Grandfather!" declared the boy, pointing to the arrows. "I did not miss! But look at Spirit Bear's arrow, it is all the way!"

Gabe chuckled, "Yeah, but it probably broke off under him," reaching to lift the lower leg and roll the animal to its back, readying to field dress it. And as he suspected, the arrow was broken, but the point was buried in the dirt, the broken shaft revealing its location. Gabe picked it up and dropped it into the quiver, then withdrew the rest of the arrow and did the same.

"You made a good shot," he said to the boy, pointing at his arrow before he plucked it out. "Here ya go, that's a lucky arrow, you need to mark that one."

"So, now we do the messy work." He looked at Antelope, "You got a knife?" The boy shook his head and Gabe reached to his sheath that hung between his shoulder blades and withdrew the smaller of his two Flemish knives, handing it to the boy. "Here ya go, you can use this one. Since your arrow struck first, you make the first cut!" The boy accepted the knife, glanced to his grandfather, smiling, then turned to the task at the carcass.

7 / RETURN

The boy, with his grandfather's help and direction, soon had the deer dressed out and deboned, the meat bundled in the hide, and turned to Gabe, grinning and proud. Gabe looked at the boy and said, "You might wanna wash up a mite in the creek, there," nodding to the shallow eddy at the edge of the bank. The boy and the old man were quick in their understanding of Gabe's sign and smattering of Shoshone.

As they walked back into camp, the bundle over Gabe's shoulder, Ezra frowned at the three, gave a slight nod that Gabe instantly understood. Gabe glanced at the boy, "You and your grandfather cut the meat, steaks and smokin' strips, and we," nodding to Ezra, "will be back."

The two friends walked to the edge of the trees that stood beside the creek bank and Ezra looked at Gabe, "Trouble's comin'," he declared.

Gabe frowned, "Yeah, I've been lookin' over my shoulder ever since we left to go huntin'. Got them 'heebie-jeebies' again?"

Ezra shrugged, "At first, I just thought it was thinkin' 'bout Spotted Eagle and the Salish comin'. But it's more than that."

"Natural or man-made?" asked Gabe. He was remembering the time that Ezra's premonition of the earthquake had saved their bacon, as well as other times when it was not a happening of nature.

"Many horses," explained Ezra.

"Let's talk to the old man," suggested Gabe, turning back to the camp.

The meat was already hanging over the flames, broiling and dripping juices into the fire, when Gabe and Ezra walked back into camp. The boy was enthused and was deftly using Gabe's knife to cut the remaining meat into long thin strips. Gabe touched the boy's shoulder, nodded, and smiled at him, then reached for a cup to pour some coffee. He looked at the old man and signed, "Tell me about this valley, this land, and where your people live."

The old man stood, looking down the valley to the south, he pointed to the southeast, "When the buffalo come, they come from there. When they leave in the season of colors, they go there." He paused, turned slightly to his right and pointed along the line of mountains that rode the west edge of the valley and ended in the wide plains beyond, "My people live there. The Snake River cuts deep in the flat lands, but our people live on both sides of the river. Four," holding up his hand with fingers extended, "five days from here."

"The *Waiilatpus*, where is their land?" asked Gabe.

Lone Bear turned to the west and pointed to the long mountain range, "They live beyond these mountains. The Snake River turns to the north and their land is beyond the Snake."

Gabe frowned, "Is their land near the Nez Percé?"

The old man put his palms together, "Beside them."

"Are they peaceful with the Nez Percé?" asked Ezra.

Lone Bear frowned, "Sometime yes, some time no. Like they are with others."

Gabe dropped his eyes to the ground, moving a rock with his toe, thinking. He looked up at Lone Bear, "The *Waiilatpus*, from the sign I saw, they went east around that point," nodding to the end of the string of mountains at their back, "but if their land is thataway," nodding to the mountains on the west, "they will probably be coming back through here on their way to their village."

Lone Bear nodded, glancing from Gabe to Ezra, and then to the youngsters. He pointed to the end of the mountains and the plains beyond, "They will go there," moving his hand from the east ridge to the west at the mouth of the long valley.

Gabe glanced that direction, then to the sun that was lowering in the west. He looked to Ezra, "I'm goin' up on that ridge behind us, take a look around, see if I can see that 'trouble' comin' that we been feelin'."

Ezra nodded, watched Gabe toss the last of the dregs of the coffee to the side and stand. He had replaced the Mongol bow in its case and now held the Ferguson rifle in his hand, Wolf stood beside him. "I'm gonna ride up that draw yonder, I think it'll take me to a point that'll be closer to the top of the ridge. I'll prob'ly have to climb a ways, but," he turned to look down the valley, "I think I'll be able to see beyond them low hills, maybe see if there's anybody out there."

Ezra nodded toward the dripping meat, "Take some o' that with you, cuz if you're climbin' that ridge, you're gonna need it!"

The mouth of the draw was a little more than a half mile from their camp by the creek, but once around the point, Gabe saw the draw become a deep canyon that led to the timbered and rocky slopes of the high peaks on the east ridge. Once into the draw, a game trail pointed into a cut that rode the shoulder of the rocky ridge he had chosen for his promontory. Gabe pointed Ebony up the trail and within just over a mile, he neared a point where he could leave Ebony, and hike to the top of the ridge.

With Wolf at his heels, he zig-zagged up the slope, crested the ridge and followed the ridge to the high point for his lookout. As he walked the narrow spine of the hilltop, he saw the north slope was thick with timber, but the south side was almost barren. Rimrock also projected on the north, and the north slope was steep, while the south was tilted at a straight angle to the bottom, making Gabe think this was a piece of slab that broke and tilted up to form the strange shape and hillside. He grinned at his own thoughts, then whispered to himself, "*Thy wondrous works declare.*"

Once at the point of the ridge, he sat down, Wolf at his side, and stretched out the scope for his look see. The wide valley, deep in tall grass, moved like the waves of the ocean, but was split by the tree and brush lined stream that pointed directly down the middle. He saw some antelope in the distance, returning from the stream and moving toward the lee side of the mountains. But he lifted his scope to the end of the eastern line of timber topped hills. At the southernmost point, there was a shadow ridge of smaller but mostly bald hills, that made the long line appear to be split.

As he focused the scope on the low point between the two, he saw movement. A long line of riders, many horses, most driven, and they were moving east to west. Gabe frowned, for it was evident there was ample water and greenery at the mouth of the valley that paralleled the one where they were camped and it was late in the day, so why would they pass the lush valley and keep moving? Unless they were pursued. The valley to the west was also more fertile and was lush with greenery showing there was ample water. Perhaps they were aiming for that, but that was two, three hours or more, further, and they were moving slow which would say they were tired or had wounded among them.

He turned his scope to the camp below him, saw Ezra and the three Paiute, nothing appeared to be amiss and the smoke from the fire was dispersed in the tall cottonwoods above the cookfire. Yet the camp was not very defensible.

He turned the scope back to the riders, then moved it ahead of the leaders, looking for any advance scouts. Then he spotted two riders, rounding the point at the end of the eastern line of mountains. *They're coming up the valley!* Although he knew the creek in the valley bottom was ample for their needs, it was not more than ten, twelve feet across and no more than a foot deep, what he did not know was this creek, like several others in the area, petered out in the flats where the dry plains absorbed all the water and the creek became nothing more than a dry gravel bed.

Another quick glance to the camp below him and Gabe came to his feet and with Wolf at his side, angled down the slope to where Ebony was tethered, slipping, and sliding all the way. He swung aboard the black and turned to the game trail that led from the draw and rode into the camp. He slid to a stop and said, "Hurry! We need to leave! The *Waiilatpus* are coming back!" Everyone worked quickly, Gabe and Ezra rigging the horse and mule and saddling Ezra's bay. Lone Bear and the youngsters gathered the smoking meat and rack and their few belongings and scattered the coals, using the coffeepot to douse the hot ones. They covered the cookfire remains with dirt and leaves, did as much as they could to eradicate any sign of their being there and Gabe lifted Minnow on Ebony, Ezra took the boy, and Lone Bear climbed aboard the grey pack horse.

Gabe led the way back to the game trail that pointed them into the deeper gorge and he looked at Ezra, "It looks like there's a basin at the head of this canyon. You take 'em there and I'll see what I can do to hide our trail."

He lifted Minnow to her grandfather and turned Ebony back toward the mouth of the canyon. He hurriedly went to where they had taken the mule deer, chased off a pair of mangy coyotes and retrieved two of the lower legs from beside the gut-pile. He swung back aboard the big black, saw Wolf snatch a bone, and rode back to their campsite. He moved Ebony back and forth across their tracks, then into the creek, repeated it several times, then turned to the trail that led to the draw and the deeper canyon. He stepped down beside the tracks and pushed Ebony before him. With a branch of the cottonwood heavy with leaves, he swished it back and forth to wipe out the obvious sign of the horses, then used the hooves of the deer to overstep the remaining sign. He worked fast, knowing it would not fool a skilled tracker, but if it would prevent a casual glance from giving them away, then it would be worth it. The *Waiilatpus* had no reason to suspect anyone had survived and had horses, and they probably would not come this far up the valley, but Gabe was cautious, especially when there were vulnerable children involved.

8 / INFILTRATION

The sun had already dropped below the western mountains, the colors had faded from the sky and the long shadows of dusk were stretching to their greatest length before they would disappear into the darkness. The moon was waxing toward full but had a long way to go to get there, but the half that showed, gave just enough light for Ebony to pick his steps. Gabe had given the surefooted stallion his head and knew he would follow close after Wolf who padded quietly up the trace of a game trail that followed the bottom of the canyon. The canyon bent around two huge rock outcroppings that stood as silent sentinels to the upper reaches of the mountain basin. The wind whispered through the maze, occasionally sounding with a shriek that added mystery to the dark trek and reminded Gabe of the catacombs in the bowels of Paris that he visited with his father.

With sheer cliffs and rockslides on his left, dense black timber on his right, he was surprised when the canyon split and offered a small basin where the others had pitched camp. Gabe stepped down and loosened the girth on Ebony to let him join the other horses at the grass.

Ezra noticed his friend did not strip the gear from his horse and looked at Gabe as he turned, then dropped his eyes and let his shoulders slump in resignation. "Somethin' tells me we're goin' somewhere," he mumbled just loud enough for Gabe to hear.

Gabe chuckled, nodded, "Have to, you know how it is."

"Ummhmm, I know," answered Ezra as he followed Gabe to join the others. Gabe sat down on a flat rock and looked at Lone Bear, "How many young people do you think the *Waiilatpus* took?"

The old man squirmed on his haunches, looked up at Gabe and with one hand extended, "Perhaps one hand," all the fingers extended on his open hand, "maybe one or two more." He glanced at Antelope, nodding, "His sister, Morning Sun, was taken, and her friends. Perhaps one or two young men, but most were girls. The *Waiilatpus* use them as slaves or take them as extra wives."

When the word slave was signed and used, Gabe unconsciously glanced at Ezra, saw the anger flare, and back at Lone Bear. "We are going to go near their

camp, see if the captives can be taken, and some horses. We will leave the pack horse and mule with you.
If we do not return, they are yours, the supplies also."

"You would go against so many of the *Waiilatpus?*"
asked Lone Bear.

"We do not go to fight, but to steal the captives and
horses. If they fight, then we will fight, but hopefully
we can get in and get out without fighting."

Lone Bear frowned, slowly shaking his head, "Why
would you do this? They are not your children."

Ezra stepped forward, "We just don't like the idea
of anyone taken and made a slave. Ain't right."

Lone Bear looked from Ezra to Gabe, then replied,
"I will stay with the young ones and if you do not
return, we will wait one day, then if the *Waiilatpus* are
gone, we will start for our home."

Gabe nodded, glanced at Ezra who also nodded,
then back at Lone Bear. "Good." He glanced at the
moon, saw that most of the clouds and cleared away
the stars studded the sky, but there were patches of
blackness that showed the presence of other clouds
and Gabe unconsciously nodded, thinking the
movement of the clouds could be to their advantage. He started for Ebony, motioned for Wolf to
follow and tightened the girth and stepped aboard.
He waited for Ezra to quickly saddle the bay and
as soon as he swung aboard, the two started back
down the canyon.

Ezra spoke softly, "You have any idea what we're gonna be doin'?"

"None at all. We'll just have to play it as it comes."

"I really don't think them *Waiilatpus* are very good at playin'."

"You're right about that, but as far as I could tell, they looked to be either very tired, or they've been in a fight and some of 'em are wounded. They weren't movin' none too fast."

"A fight huh, who with?" asked Ezra, looking at Gabe as he came alongside. They had broken from the canyon and were at the mouth of the deep draw, shielded from the distant camp of the *Waiilatpus* by a low rising finger ridge.

"I think they mighta run into our Salish friends."

Ezra looked at Gabe with a frown that slowly faded, "That mighta been bad for both of 'em."

"That's what I'm thinkin'. If they've taken a beating from Spotted Eagle and his men, they might be a touch on the skittish side. So, we might keep that in mind as we decide what to do and how to do it."

They pushed into the wide valley but stayed near the edge of the eastern ridge of foothills. Gabe had guessed the *Waiilatpus* would make their camp on the far side of a small flat-top butte that stood apart from the lower line of hills that shadowed the easternmost line. They covered the five miles in the light of the moon and kept to the dark side of the butte. As they neared, Gabe motioned to Ezra that he was climbing the butte, to look down on the camp. Ezra nodded, stepped down and took the reins of the black as Gabe slipped the Ferguson from the scabbard and stepped down. With a quick glance at Ezra, a hand motion to Wolf, Gabe followed the zig-zag trail behind Wolf.

Rim rock and loose shale circled the crest of the butte like a crown of black basalt. Wolf easily mounted the obstacle, but Gabe had to more carefully pick his steps to avoid kicking a chunk loose to send it rattling down the slope. Once atop, he moved in a crouch to the far edge, bellied down and looked at the camp below. The dim glowing coals of two cookfires winked whenever the night breeze drifted through the camp. The top of the butte was about four hundred fifty feet higher than the camp and put Gabe too far away to see any detail. He gave it a thorough once over and motioned Wolf off the butte.

He joined Ezra at the bottom and softly reported, "They're on the other side alright, spread out a bit, couldn't tell about captives or much else. The horses are at this edge, two picket lines stretched out. From what I could tell, a lot more horses than warriors." Gabe saw a nearby cluster of flat rock, stepped closer and lifted his foot to the edge of one, thinking to rest a moment, but once the weight of his foot hit the stone, it exploded with the pffft of rattles! Gabe jerked back, the horses spooked and jerked at the reins, but Ezra held tight. Even Wolf jumped straight up and came down growling.

"Holy smokes!" muttered Gabe, looking back at the rocks, now about ten feet away. From under the edge, a big rattlesnake had shown himself as he coiled and readied for a strike. His head was lifted, his tongue flipping in and out, and his upper coil moving side to side as the long rattles clattered next to the rock.

"I hate snakes! If we weren't so close to them *Waiilatpus*, I'd shoot him with every pistol we got!" growled Ezra.

Gabe was breathing fast, never taking his eyes off the snake, and said, "Wait, wait, I've an idea." He lifted his rifle slowly, then glanced at Ezra, "You move that way, I'll go this way," nodding to his left. "Use the butt of your rifle to push his head down and pin it. Then we can take him alive."

Ezra jerked his head toward Gabe, "Alive! What for you wanna do that? You crazy?"

"If we can get him, maybe one or two more, we can use them to distract the *Waiilatpus* while we take their horses or captives."

"Ummhmm, you have done lost your mind!"

"C'mon, help me," pleaded Gabe.

"Alright, but I'm gonna be up on top o' that there rock!"

With Ezra atop the rock, and Gabe coming from the side, the snake tried to watch both, looking for a chance to sink his fangs deep into the threat, but Ezra was too high. His long Lancaster rifle was just the right length and when he lowered the butt near the rattler, the snake struck out and Ezra pinned the head down against the flat of the rock. He looked at Gabe, "Alright, he's pinned, now what?"

"Lemme get him. When I do, take off your shirt."

"What'chu want my shirt for?"

"You'll see," answered Gabe, slowly approaching the pinned rattler that was trying to coil around the stock of the rifle. Gabe grabbed it just behind the head and nodded to Ezra to take away the rifle. With his free hand, Gabe caught the snake close to the tail and held it away from his body, watching it and Ezra both as Ezra slipped his buckskin shirt over his head. Ezra dropped the shirt on the flat rock, spreading it out and Gabe lay the snake down, motioned for Ezra to fold the shirt over and bundle up the snake.

Gabe had no sooner released the snake than another rattle sounded almost at his feet, but in one quick move, Gabe was atop the rock and looking down at the other snake. It took some doing, but by the time they were finished, they had three big rattlers bundled in the buckskin shirt and the men were back at the horses, planning their next moves.

9 / HAUNT

Gabe stepped back and admired his work. He grinned as he looked at Ezra, "If you could only see yourself now! You're plum scary!"

Ezra glowered at his friend, then picked up his war club and rifle. He hung the powder horn and possibles pouch from the rifle and turned away from Gabe to start around the far end of the flat top butte. Wolf trotted beside Ezra, with just a quick glance back at Gabe.

Gabe started around the opposite end of the butte, his belt bristling with both the double-barreled saddle pistols and his Bailes over/under swivel pistol. The tomahawk hung at his side, his knives at his back and his Ferguson carried loosely in his hand at his side. He trotted around the butte, slowing as he drew nearer the sleeping *Waiilatpus*. He dropped to his knee, then down to all fours. With the tall grasses, an occasional clump of sage and cholla cacti, for cover, he still moved at a snail's pace, rifle cradled in his arms as he used his elbows and knees to move. The smell of smoke, bear grease, stale bodies, and blood, told Gabe he was near. He paused, slowly lifted his head and pushed aside the tall grass to look at the camp.

He was about thirty feet from the closest figure, a man that sat cross legged, head hanging as he dozed. Gabe looked around the perimeter of the camp for another guard, saw one near the horses and knew Ezra would take care of that one, for he too was seated and dozing. Gabe searched for any figure that could be a captive, saw two that lay back to back, probably tied together, but saw no others. Only single forms, lying on and under blankets, making the usual sounds of sleeping men, snoring, snorting, mumbling, but nothing that was disturbing. The common night sounds of cicadas, a distant coyote, and a nighthawk soaring high above with his pee-yah midnight cry, could be heard.

Gabe slowly moved closer to the dozing guard, laid his rifle aside and rose with knife in hand as quietly as a shadow. One step brought him behind the man and as he reached out to grab his mouth, the man jerked up and turned, but Gabe was quicker and cupped his hand over the man's mouth and brought the knife behind him, burying it in the man's back. He kicked and struggled, but when Gabe twisted the knife and drew it toward the man's spine, the guard went limp, and Gabe slowly lowered him to the ground.

Gabe dropped to one knee, wiped the blood from his knife and slipped it back into its sheath. He reached for the rifle, glanced toward the other guard, but he was nowhere to be seen. Gabe grinned slightly, knowing Ezra had done his job. Gabe stayed unmoving, then stepped to where the guard had been seated, and took his place. He looked around the camp, watching for any movement and doing a search for any figures that might be captives. His eyes rested on the couple that were back to back, saw the one facing him had her eyes open and watching him. He lifted his head slowly to nod to the girl, smiled, then slowly rose, and started toward her.

He turned slightly to look at the edge of the hill above where the horses were picketed, saw a shadow move, grinned, and dropped to one knee beside the girl. With the dim moonlight, he hoped she could see as he signed, "Lone Bear sent us. I will cut you free, you run there," nodding to the end of the butte, "our horses are there. Wait for us."

The girl nodded, and Gabe slipped his knife from its sheath and quickly cut their bonds. The other girl turned, wide-eyed, when her bonds were cut, but the first girl whispered to her. They slowly rose and quickly moved to the end of the butte. Gabe stepped back near some rocks, waiting for Ezra to make his move and with a quick glance his way, Gabe raised his rifle to his shoulder, eared back the hammer and waited.

Everything split the quiet of the darkness at once. Ezra threw the rattlesnakes into the middle of the sleepers, two landing atop sleeping forms. Wolf lifted his head to a mournful howl and Ezra screamed a blood-curdling war cry! Ezra stood on a flat rock that rested on a slight shoulder of the butte, screamed, swung his war club over his head and stood with the club held high, rearing back and screaming. Gabe had painted Ezra's black visage with white streaks of clay that made him look like a living skeleton. His face showed white as a skull, his arms and legs like the long bones and his chest painted like the rib cage of a dead man. He jumped, screamed, waving his war club.

The *Waiilatpus* sprang from their blankets, screaming and jumping because of the slithering and rattling snakes at their feet. They pointed, screamed, ran around crashing into one another, then when Ezra screamed, they stood stock still, stared, then remembered the snakes and several snatched at their blankets, others left their blankets behind and they ran for their horses. But before they reached the animals, the horses spooked at both the snakes and the Wolf and the screaming banshee on the mountain, jerked at the cut tethers and finding themselves unhindered, reared up, kicked out, screamed and turned and ran into the night.

Some of the warriors started to turn back, but another scream from the ghostly apparition on the hillside convinced them to run after their horses. Within moments, the campsite was nothing but abandoned blankets, smoldering coals that stunk with burning blankets that had been tossed at snakes but landed on the coals. Gabe whistled to Ezra, and Wolf and his friend was soon at his side. They wasted no time getting to their horses, but the startled girls were hesitant to move after seeing Ezra, even though Ezra had replaced his britches and shirt. Gabe spoke in Shoshone and sign, saying he was a friend with paint. Even though the girls did not know the men, and neither had ever seen a black man, when Gabe had said Lone Bear sent them, they hoped they were friends, knowing that whatever they were, it would be better than being a captive of the *Waiilatpus*. The men swung aboard the horses, gave the girls a hand, and left the butte behind as they took off at a canter, anxious to put some distance between them and the *Waiilatpus*.

As they neared the mouth of the canyon that held their camp, Gabe pointed to the creek below, "That looks like some of the horses you ran off, don't ya' think?"

"Mebbe so. Shall we take a look?"

"We could use some horses, so, yeah. I don't think the *Waiilatpus* will be comin' anytime soon."

They separated, approaching the horses from both sides. There were three horses, grazing on the greener grass by the creek and had probably been attracted by the stream. They had run for most of five miles from the butte and would have sought out both water and graze. The men spoke softly until the girl with Gabe squirmed and slid to the ground. She motioned to the other girl, and as Gabe and Ezra approached on horseback, the girls moved closer on foot, hands outstretched and speaking to the animals as they moved.

The horses were easily caught, each having a braided rawhide halter with a dangling lead after they had been picketed. The girls swung aboard their chosen horses, led the third and nodded to Gabe to lead the way. The familiar trail was easily followed in the moonlight and they soon came to the camp where Lone Bear sat in the dark, watching them approach. He stood and stepped from the shadows as they neared. A broad smile split his face when he saw the girls and the first girl slid from her mount and ran into the arms of Lone Bear.

The old man looked at Gabe, "This is Morning Sun, my granddaughter, the sister of Antelope and Minnow."

Gabe and Ezra quickly stripped the gear from the horses, rubbed them down and tethered them near the grass, beside the three new additions and the pack animals. They walked back to the others and sat down, looking at a happy old man and his granddaughter. He nodded to the other girl, "This is Walks Tall, Morning Sun's friend."

Gabe and Ezra nodded, then Gabe looked at Lone Bear, "Did they tell you if there were other captives?"

The old man dropped his head, then lifted it to look at his new friends, sadness and anger painted his wrinkled face, fire flared in his eyes. "The girls were used and killed, the boys were tortured and killed. These were not harmed. Morning Sun convinced her captors they were unclean and should not be touched." Gabe shook his head at the word of the death of the captives yet chuckled within himself that the girls had used their womanly times to save their lives. Although they knew it would be temporary and they risked being killed outright, they gambled and won. He glanced at the girls then back to Lone Bear, "Had the *Waiilatpus* been in a fight?"

He nodded, "Yes. They attacked a band of people coming to hunt buffalo, but the others fought bravely and turned the *Waiilatpus* away."

"Do they know who the others were? What tribe?"

"They do not know. But it was a large band with women and children and many warriors."

Gabe looked at Ezra, "Probably Spotted Eagle and his people."

"That's what I figgered. Hope they didn't lose too many. After their set-to with the Blackfoot last year, they don't need any more losses."

Gabe looked to Lone Bear, "I don't know if the *Waiilatpus* will follow us or not. They were running in every direction and chasing their horses and such. But I reckon they're not too happy 'bout what happened. So, we should get some rest while we can and be ready to move out in a hurry if need be."

"You sleep. I will watch," declared the old man.

Gabe glanced at Ezra, then back to Lone Bear. "That will be good."

10 / DEPARTURE

The morning sun had yet to reach into the deep basin when Gabe returned from his time with the Lord. Ezra had left early and had yet to return, but the others had already set about fixing the morning meal. The two girls, Morning Sun and Walks Tall, had taken over the duties from Lone Bear and he sat beside his grandson, Antelope and the girls worked around the fire. They knew nothing about the coffeepot and how to prepare the morning brew, but Lone Bear had learned quickly and directed the girls at the task.

When Gabe walked back into camp with Wolf at his side, the girls looked up smiling, and Morning Sun pointed to the coffeepot that was bubbling at its spout, "We made your drink!" she declared excitedly. Gabe was picking up on the inflections and pronunciations of the Paiute tongue and its similarity to the language of the Shoshone, and mostly understood what was

said, but the girl's pointing and speaking told him all
he needed to understand. He smiled, nodding and
went to the pot to pour himself some, but when he
saw it boiling out the spout, he sat it aside, removed
the top, and poured in a bit of cold water to settle the
grounds, then poured his cup full.

He sat down, took a sip of the coffee, struggled to
swallow the stiff brew, but smiled at the girls, nodding. It was considerably stronger that what he was
used to, but he had to show his appreciation for their
efforts. He looked at Lone Bear, who had noticed his
reaction and was grinning, then asked, "Tell me more
about your people."

Lone Bear looked to the ground, used a stick to
poke around and gather his thoughts, then began. "In
the days of summer, the buffalo have migrated to this
land," he pointed with the stick down canyon, "to have
their young. They move around this land, grazing and
nursing the young. It is not until the young can keep
up with the herd that they leave to go south for the
winter. My people live by the Snake River and at this
time, after the buffalo calves are on the ground and
growing strong, my people come to the north to take
our meat for the winter."

"Does the entire village come?" asked Gabe, knowing that with some of the Plains tribes, the buffalo
hunt is a time for the entire village to be involved.

"No, many stay at the place of our village. Many

families have planted crops, the three sisters, corn, squash, and beans, to prepare for winter and those need to be tended. Each hunt, different ones go, sometimes it is the entire family, sometimes just the hunters. There are as many that stay behind as those that come on the hunt."

"Had there been any buffalo taken by your people?"

"No, we had just made this camp the day before we were attacked. The buffalo are at that," pointing to the east, "end of the plains."

Gabe frowned, thinking of the Salish and Spotted Eagle. If they had been in a battle with the *Waiilat-pus*, they could already be returning to their village, but if there were enough to remain and hunt, they would be preparing for the hunt and would probably be expecting to see Gabe and Ezra. He thought a moment, looked around the camp and noticed that Ezra's bay was missing. He frowned, looked down the canyon trail and asked Lone Bear, "Did you see Black Buffalo leave?"

"He took his horse and went down the trail. I was still in my blankets and he said nothing."

It was then that Gabe heard the clatter of horse's hooves on the rocky trail and knew Ezra was returning, but to be sure, he reached for his rifle and motioned to Wolf to scout the trail. Within a few moments, Wolf turned back to Gabe, no alarm showing, and the bobbing head of the bay showed from the edge of the trees. Ezra was grinning as he came into view and was soon at the camp, stepping down from his horse.

"I had to get rid of that white clay you painted me up with, it was dryin' out, cakin' up and I needed to wash it off! Didn't like lookin' like a skeleton!"

"You went clear down to the creek?" asked a flabbergasted Gabe. "What about the *Waiilatpus?*"

Ezra grinned, "Ahh, you were worried about me!" He chuckled, then explained, "I took your scope and made a good look around 'fore I showed myself. There's no sign of 'em, so I reckon they done left the country!"

"That's good," responded Gabe, reaching for another cup for his friend. Ezra picked up the coffeepot and poured himself a cup, his forehead wrinkling when he saw the black brew stream into the cup. He glanced at Gabe with a frown, and Gabe explained, "The girls fixed it for us, wasn't that nice of 'em?"

Ezra nodded, smiling and looked at the girls with a broad smile as he lifted his cup in a bit of a salute to them, then took a sip, forced it down and sat across the fire from Gabe and Lone Bear. The old man grinned at Ezra, appreciative of his response to the girls.

Gabe looked at Lone Bear, "So, if the *Waiilatpus* are gone, I reckon you'll be wanting to get back to your village and let the others know what happened, right?"

"Yes, I must tell them," muttered a somber Lone Bear, the weight of his people showing as he sat with slumped shoulders.

"Would you like us to go with you? Just to be safe?" asked Ezra.

Lone Bear looked up at Ezra, then shook his head, "If the *Waiilatpus* are gone, there is no need. We have horses now and you have helped us, and we are grateful, but we must return."

Ezra looked at Gabe, "You know, if those *Waiilatpus* didn't return to their camp, there might be some things left that could be used by Lone Bear and the girls, you know, blankets, maybe some weapons."

"Might be, at least we can take a look," replied Gabe, then looking at Lone Bear, "We were on our way to meet the Salish village that came for a buffalo hunt. We think they were the ones that the *Waiilatpus* ran into and had a fight. They are our friends and we were going to share in the hunt, so, if you and the youngsters will be alright, we'll go east to meet them."

The sun crested the eastern mountains as the small group came from the timbered canyon into the grassy flats of the valley. Lone Bear had Antelope before him as the two rode beside Gabe, with the grey pack horse following close behind. They were followed by the two girls, with Morning Sun holding her sister, Minnow, before her, on one of the other two horses recovered from the *Waiilatpus* herd. Ezra had a lead on the mule because of the mule's unpredictable temperament around strange horses and rode at the end of the group. It was a pleasant morning, the sky devoid of clouds and showing a brilliant cobalt blue. The warm sun brought warmth to their shoulders and gave a brightness to the day. The well-rested horses were stepping lively, apparently happy to be on the move again.

As they neared the flat-top butte that hid the campsite of the *Waiilatpus*, Gabe motioned Ezra to scout it out and took the lead of the mule as he moved past. "We'll wait here at the tree line, just in case."

Ezra nodded, kicked the bay to a canter and quickly covered the short distance to the butte. He tethered his bay at the trees, then with rifle in hand, slowly picked his way around the east side of the butte to view the campsite. As expected, it was abandoned, and showed no evidence of the return of the *Waiilatpus*. Blankets were scattered, Ezra saw two bows and quivers that had been kicked aside, probably when the rattlesnakes hit the middle of the camp and everyone scattered. He chuckled at the memory, but made a complete circle of the camp, looking for any sign of the return of the warriors. All the tracks showed men running in one direction, away from the scene of terror.

He shook his head, knowing that most of the native people were superstitious about the dead, with most refusing to return to the place where they believed the spirits of the dead were seen. Some would even destroy the lodge where someone had died, usually burying their possessions, and even killing their horses to be buried with them. Ezra finished his survey, returned to his horse and turned toward the others, stood in his stirrups, and waved his neckerchief in the air to signal them to come.

When the others rode into the camp, they reined up to look, scanning the refuse and searching for anything of use, but Walks Tall noticed the body of the guard killed by Gabe, ravens and two turkey buzzards were fighting over the remains, but there was something about the form that Walks Tall recognized. She gigged her horse toward the scene, scattering the birds, and when she recognized the figure, she spat on the body, and reined her horse away. She looked at Morning Sun, nodding with a look of anger that covered her face.

Morning Sun glanced at Gabe, said, "He is one that used and killed our friends."

There was nothing Gabe could say, but he dropped his eyes and stepped down from Ebony, to begin walking through the camp. He picked up a quiver and a bow, handed it to Lone Bear and another that he handed to Morning Sun. She passed it to Walks Tall, looked at Gabe and explained, "She is much better with the bow. I believe she will one day be a warrior."

Gabe nodded, "That is good. My woman is a war leader among her people, the Shoshone."

Morning Sun smiled, "We have some Shoshone among our people. One of our leaders, Winnemucca, was born a Shoshone, but married a *Kuyuidika* Paiute and became a Paiute!"

They gave Lone Bear and the girls the rest of the smoked meat from the deer taken by Antelope and said their good-byes. Lone Bear encouraged them to visit his village, "Your names will be sung around our fires and you will always be welcome in our village." The old man nodded, extended his hand to bid his goodbye and turned away, to start across the wide plains. It would be about a three-day ride for the group, but it would be through friendly and familiar country, yet with a sad message to share.

11 / WAIILATPUS

Pale Eagle was the shaman or medicine man of the *Waiilatpus* and traveled with the band led by Tawatoy and Tauitau, young warriors gaining in stature and honors among the warrior societies and were thought to be eventual prospects for head chief of the *Waiilatpus*. Whenever the *Waiilatpus* sent a party to trade or raid, they had to have a medicine man to conjure up the power needed for success. But now, Pale Eagle stood before the two young warriors with many others behind them and faced their questions and accusations.

Tawatoy glared at the shaman as he paced back and forth before him, "You said our power was good! You said our weapons would run with the blood of our enemies! But the blood of our warriors has pooled on the ground beside their rotting bodies!" His accusations elicited many cries and screams from the band of warriors behind the leaders. Several showed wounds of the fights, one had a leg so swollen he could not walk, and the color of putrid flesh was crawling up in his leg. The puncture marks of the flying rattlesnakes showed on the swollen and discolored leg, at least four sets of fang marks showed below the knee. But others had been struck in the face and neck and had not lived to see this day.

"You were told to make trade with the Paiute, not slaughter them," countered Pale Eagle, glaring defiantly at the young warriors. Although almost twice their age, and with many years of serving the people, a shaman is only as good as his last boast and when their power is not as foretold, they are in danger of losing their position and often their life.

"Hah! You said we should trade for their goods, but we took everything they would trade, and more! We took their horses and their women and gave nothing in return!"

"Aiiieee," shouted Tauitau, the more militant of the two men. "We destroyed the Paiute, but when you told us our power was great and we would kill the band of Flathead hunters, you told us wrong! They were ready for us! We lost many of our warriors because your power is gone!" Tauitau and Tawatoy had long been rivals, both exceptional warriors among a people who were known for their fearless fighters and valiant warriors. Tawatoy was thought to be the next chief and in line for the main chief of all the *Liksiyu* people, a people that prided themselves on their dominance of their land and the neighboring tribes. Considered a proud and haughty people, even their name meant *superior people.* Many weaker tribes paid them tribute.

"You said you sweat, prayed, chanted and the power of the spirits were with you! Yet, the spirit of the dead Paiute came upon us in the night, driving us from our camp with snakes and chants as he danced with the black wolf! You have no power! You are of no use to us!" declared Tawatoy. His words were echoed and shouted by the others, as they screamed and shouted for the blood of the shaman.

Tauitau stepped before the man who stood defiant with his buffalo skull headpiece that held a halo of eagle feathers standing straight, each one tipped with a tuft of white fur. His arms crossed over his hair pipe breast plate, leather armbands with elk teeth strained against his flexed biceps, thin wisps of grey marked the long hair that hung loosely over his shoulders. The young leader of the more hostile *Waiilatpus* drew his flint bladed knife, held it high above his head and screamed, "A shaman with no power must join the spirits that have abandoned him!"

The warriors screamed, chanted, and lifted weapons above their head to add their cries to those of their leaders, and one shouted above the others, "Give his heart to the buzzards!"

Tauitau turned to the medicine man, snarled and plunged his knife into the man's chest, twisted it, and as the medicine man's legs began to sag, Tauitau pulled the flint blade free and as the shaman fell forward, Tauitau drew the blade across the man's neck, slitting his throat from ear to ear, then let the body fall. He lifted the bloody knife overhead, and screamed, prompting answering screams from the others.

Tauitau stepped to the side of his co-leader, Tawatoy, "We should have another shaman."

"We will return to the village. Our people are allied with the Nez Percé and the Umatillas. There are many that would join us on another raid against those that turned us away," declared Tawatoy. "And there are others that have studied under the shamans that would join us also."

Tauitau looked at his rival, "Why would we want someone from the lesser tribes? We are *Waiilatpus*! There are none as good as us! Our leaders are weak and old, they do not have courage they once had, water flows in their veins!" he spat the words of contempt. He thought the same of the man that stood before him. Although the two men were comparable in size, Tauitau had repeatedly shown himself to be the more fierce and bold in battle, but Tawatoy had proven the wiser of the two and led with wisdom and courage. They had been matched many times in the contests of strength and stamina when the different bands gathered for trade fairs and more, but neither had bested the other repeatedly.

"We return with many horses, but we have lost warriors and now the shaman. Our chief, Big Horse, and the others may protest against our returning to raid again," stated Tawatoy.

"If they want to trade and fish, let them. I will lead the real warriors and we will go after the Salish and take their women and their horses! We will become our own band!" spat Tauitau. The division among the warriors was evident even before they had left the village on this raid, but for anyone to openly defy the leaders and take warriors away from the village against their counsel was open defiance and would be marked as hostile renegades and banned from the villages of the people.

Tawatoy dropped his head as he sat down on the log near the fire, he looked back at Tauitau, "You would do that?"

"The *Liksiyu* are known as a strong and fierce people. Would you have them make us into weak fishers and traders?"

"No, but to become a renegade and weaken our village by taking warriors away, would make our village prey for others!"

"You will have no glory, no booty, no honors, if

you do not join the Black Bear Warriors!" He spoke of what had been a somewhat secret war society among the people, but the Black Bear was not the only one. Warrior societies had long been common among the people, but never openly spoken about except by initiates.

"When we return to the village, we will seek the counsel of the elders. Then we will fast and pray, go to the sweat lodge, and have a dance. Then, if the spirits lead you, then go. But do not do this thing without being prepared," warned Tawatoy.

"We will do this," answered Tauitau. His grin told of his confidence in what he had already chosen to do and that he would go through the motions, but his mind was already set on his way.

It was mid-day the following day when Tawatoy led the band of raiders off the wide mesa of lava and dry grass, into the riverbed of the Snake River, where the three bands, the *Waiilatpus*, Nez Percé, and the Umatilla had their allied camp. The wide bend of the river, where the course turned from flowing north to the west, harbored the scattered camps. All were camped on the northeast side of the bend and nearer the river, a massive horse herd grazed on the tall grasses. The combined camp had over a hundred lodges, most were hide teepees, but there were also several brush huts and one prominent long house with a tule covering. This would be the meeting place of the combined councils, and the lodge of the chief of the *Waiilatpus*, Big Horse.

The reception was jubilant, with many of the family members rushing to greet their warriors as they rode into the village, the horse herd was shepherded at the rear of the band and as they came into the camp, those in charge of the horses, pushed the herd past the others toward the rest of the animals by the river. Big Horse, true to his name, stood almost head and shoulders over those that were near, other elders and leaders and their women, and all stood stoic as they watched the return of the raiding band. The leaders looked at the horses, noticed some of different stock and were pleased to note the warriors had captured many new horses, but they also noticed the absence of captives and that many warriors were missing.

Tawatoy and Tauitau dropped to the ground before the chief, and without any words spoken, the chief turned toward the entry of the long house, was followed closely by the elders, and then Tawatoy and Tauitau followed. The entire group was seated before a low burning fire, and blankets that had covered shoulders were now dropped and everyone settled to a comfortable position, most with legs crossed before them, as they sat looking across the small fire at the leaders of the returning raiding party.

Big Horse said simply, "Tell us," speaking directly

to Tawatoy, and not looking at Tauitau.

The young warrior began with his report of the Paiute village. "Pale Eagle said his power was great and our power resided with us. We chose to take the village by force and destroyed our enemies! We took many horses, several captives, and all their goods," declared Tawatoy, proudly as he glanced from one of the elders to the others. He continued. "Pale Eagle rode at the front with us as he should, and when we saw a band of hunters, he lifted his spirit lance and said the power was good. We attacked, but they had many others waiting and came on us with power like we have never seen. They had weapons of thunder that killed from a distance greater than a bow, and they also had weapons like ours. We were turned away by their weapons of great thunder, many of our warriors had fallen, and we fled the battle. Pale Eagle's power was gone."

Before he could continue, Big Horse asked, "How many of our young warriors did you lose?"

"Three hands," replied Tawatoy, quietly with his head bowed.

"Tell us more," commanded Big Horse.

"When we camped, we were set upon by the spirit of the dead Paiute, our camp was filled with deadly flying rattlesnakes, slithering and biting everyone, and the spirit danced on the hillside, waving his war club and dancing with a giant black wolf!" declared

Tawatoy, as the telling of the tale renewed the fear he felt when he was there. He shook his head, his hands trembling, and continued, "Our horses had spooked and torn free, for they too were afraid, we chased after them and caught most of them, but some of our warriors died from the snake bite and some were killed by the spirit!"

"How many?"

"Two were killed by the spirit, three by the snakes. And Pale Eagle surrendered his life. As is the custom of our people, when the shaman has lost his power, he must also lose his blood."

"How many snakes?"

Tawatoy looked at Tauitau, then back at the chief, "At least two double hands!"

The chief frowned, "And this spirit, what did he look like?"

"Like death itself. He was nothing but bones that shown in the dark and the wolf that was beside him was as big as a horse!"

The elders squirmed in place, uncomfortable with the talk of spirits and giant animals and snakes. Most were wide eyed and watched as both Tawatoy and Tauitau showed fear in their eyes by the telling of the tale and Tawatoy's hands shook as he spoke. Big Horse looked at the others, then back at the young warriors, "We will speak of this. Go. We will talk again."

The two rivals looked at one another, stood, and started for the entry. Big Horse added, "It would be good for you to seek counsel with the shaman for your deeds."

The young men nodded and left the longhouse. Once outside, they looked at one another and Tauitau said, "I will go to my people. If you want to go to the shaman, go, but I will not," then turned his back on his rival and walked away.

12 / TRADERS

The images of Lone Bear and the girls had faded in the morning haze when Gabe and Ezra turned their mounts to the northeast to search out the Salish. The sun was high in the clear blue sky, no clouds to shield the travelers from the glaring heat. The wind had faded and with no breeze, no shade, and the dry land, travel had become a trial. Every footfall brought up a puff of dust and within the first hour, horses, men and gear were covered with the powdery alkaline dust. They let the horses plod at their own pace, heads bobbing and snorting to rid their nostrils of the dry dust. The men lifted their neckerchiefs to cover their mouths and noses, lifted the collar to keep the dust from their necks and hunkered down with hat brims pulled low. They were hot, sweaty and the smell of unwashed bodies stifled their breathing.

Gabe saw through squinted eyes a steam cloud

rising from between two buttes and he frowned, wondering if what he saw was a mirage, low lying clouds, or really a steam cloud. He spat the dust from his mouth, and turned to call to Ezra over his shoulder, "Is that a steam cloud yonder?" pointing with his uplifted arm.

"Looks like it! You thinkin' hot springs?"

"Yeah, might not feel as good as a cold dip, but could be good on sore muscles!"

"I'm game!" declared Ezra.

As they reined into the flat between the buttes, there was the distinct smell of Sulphur, but a small stream showed clear as it broke from the willows. A slight rise showed white with the minerals from the springs, and the men were reminded of the many geysers and springs they saw at the Shoshone grand encampment. They reined up at the edge of the flat below the springs, and after they tested the water in the stream for temperature and taste, they tethered the animals within reach of the clear water and the grassy flat. Several clouds had drifted in from the north, offering a bit of respite from the glaring sun, and distant thunder told of a possible storm.

Gabe looked at the clouds as he loosened the girth on Ebony and the packhorse, "I think we could get us in a bit of a soak 'fore that blows in and cools things off."

"Yeah, but there ain't a tree within miles fer protection!" answered Ezra.

"Aww, didn't you see that cut back around that butte yonder. Looked like it'd give shelter for us an' the horses!" declared Gabe.

"Then let's get rid o' some o' this dust!" responded Ezra, finishing tending the horse and mule. He had a blanket in one hand, his rifle in the other and started for the hot springs. Gabe was right behind him. They paused at the edge of the crystal-clear pool, admiring the turquoise color of the deep water. Ezra bent down to test the temperature, smiled over his shoulder to Gabe and said, "Feels 'bout right. But, I'm gonna be a little cautious." He saw Gabe nod approval, then shucked his moccasins, belt with the pistol and tomahawk and knife, lay his hat atop the pile and slowly waded into the edge of the pool. He tip-toed, adjusting to the temperature and soon sat down. He leaned back and splashed down into the water, letting the hot springs cover him completely.

Gabe chuckled as he watched his friend, saw a thin film of dust float on the surface, and shook his head. He sat down on an outcrop of rock, lay his rifle over his lap and looked around the area. Above the springs there appeared to be another splotch of white deposit, indicating another hot springs about a half mile above this one. The rolling hills climbed slowly to some higher peaks further east, Gabe guessed about ten or twelve miles distant. To the south, the flat lands, showing patches of deep grass, wider swaths of bunch grass and sagebrush, seemed to go on forever. Yet in the middle of it all, a random butte rose as if placed there as an afterthought with leftover goods from the hand of the Creator. It was a vast land, buffalo land, abundant with game. Antelope, coyote, wolves, jackrabbits, rattlesnakes, and a multitude of smaller creatures, made this vast flat their home.

"Hey! Your turn!" declared Ezra as he walked, dripping from the pool. He had left his buckskins on for the sole reason of ridding them of the alkali dust that could destroy the leather, but then stripped them off to get the grime from his body. Gabe followed his example, knowing the buckskin would dry better as he wore them and kept them stretched and flexible, than if they were left to dry in the air. He took his time, enjoying the hot mineral water and once the buckskins were shed, soaped himself with the lye soap, washing the grime from his hair and stubble as well. He soon climbed from the pool, wrung out his clothing and slipped them back on, put on his dry moccasins, and was ready to go, just as the thunder rolled across the sky to warn of the coming storm.

They hastily mounted up and took to the trail around the point to the undercut Gabe had spotted earlier. A long ridge with rimrock at its crest, bent to the west and into a long wide draw. The undercut of the rimrock was probably the result of a high-water wash out, but now promised shelter from the coming storm. The overhang was about fifteen feet deep and fifty to sixty feet wide. The underside of the overhang, blackened by cookfires of the past, was solid rock and extended into the belly of the ridge. There was a pile of wood, looking like driftwood from floodwaters, stacked at one end. They stripped the gear from the horses, stacked the packs against the wall, and tethered the animals.

In a short while, they had a small fire going and the coffeepot heating. With the fresh meat given to Lone Bear, they had to make do with jerky and some dried camas bulbs, but it would be enough for now. They arranged some rocks for seats and settled in, leaning back against the wall of the undercut and looking out at the darkening sky and seeing the wind that always precedes the storm, kicking up dust clouds. The storm was coming from the north, or behind the bluff with the overhang, and the dust was blowing over the top of the butte. Then the rain came, sprinkling at first, then pouring with the wind howling and blowing.

Gabe reached for the coffeepot, lifted the lid and poured in a handful of fresh grounds, flipped the lid closed and set it back on the rock beside the flames. He leaned back, just as he heard, "Hello the camp!" come from the darkness of the storm.

"Hello!" he answered, standing, and reaching for his rifle.

"Can we come in? We're friendly!"

"Come on, keep your hands where I can see 'em!" answered Gabe. He motioned to Ezra to go near the horses and stand ready.

Two men, leading their horses, came into the overhang. The one in the lead, doffed his hat and slapped it against his leg to rid it of water, then looked up at Gabe. He was an average sized man, buckskins, full beard of dusty brown, receding hairline but no grey, and a stern expression from under a heavy brow and deep-set eyes. "Howdy! I'm Alexander Ross, and this here's Bertram Quigley, and I couldna' hardly believe my eyes when we saw you round that point yonder. Never expected to see no white men in this country!" he glanced over at Ezra, saw his stern visage and the ready rifle, frowned, and said, "Uh, well, you know what I mean. Didn't expect to see none but natives!"

The men had their saddle horses and one pack horse and Gabe motioned for them to put them with the others, which they did, but the one man kept talking all the while. "We been working our way southeast, meetin' different tribes, lookin' to do some tradin' in the future. Been in the territory for nigh unto a year now, lookin' to go back north a mite."

The two quickly finished with the horses and walked back to the fire, anxious to dry off. "Say, is that coffee I smell?" asked the one called Bertram. He was about the same height as the other man, but more on the lean side. Black hair that hung to his shoulders, full beard and thick eyebrows and piercing black eyes, spoke of a Spaniard heritage, but the name didn't fit.

Gabe answered, "Yessir, it is. Get yourself a cup and we'll pour it up just as soon as its ready!"

"I'm for that! Ross here, Scotsman that he is, favors tea! And I've had more'n that than I care to, prob'ly 'nuff to last a lifetime!" declared Bertram.

As the men found themselves a seat, Ross looked to Gabe, "You fellas traders?"

"No, just travelers. Met some traders recently though, both Hudson's Bay and Northwest. You with those outfits?"

"No, no. I'm actually scoutin' for some fellas that are talking about formin' a new company. Seems several o' them money people got together in the Beaver Club, up Montreal way and put their heads together and decided they needed someone to scout out new territory."

He paused, frowned, "But you said you ran into some traders from Hudson's and Northwest?"

Gabe nodded slowly, glanced at Ezra who had taken his seat beside Gabe and said, "That's right, 'bout a month ago, north of here a ways." He was hesitant to say much about the set-to until he knew more about these men. Just because they talked a good story, didn't mean they could be trusted. And with the friendship of several tribes at stake, he would be a little stingy with his information. "Tell me about this 'Beaver Club', what's that?"

Ross chuckled, "It's one of those exclusive clubs in Montreal that is restricted to the membership and it's hard to get a membership, unless you know the right people and have the right money! But it's one of those places where important men, at least those that think they're important, make important decisions that affect the rest of us in one way or another. What with the rising popularity of beaver pelts and a world-wide market, especially in China, those same men want to get in on the money! So, that's why we're here, looking for good beaver country and people that are willing to make trade with us."

"So, you're movin' in on Hudson's Bay territory?" asked Ezra.

"No, not especially. Their country is further north, although they've made a few forays into the French Louisiana country."

"What about Northwest then?" asked Gabe.

"Now, that's a different story. They want to open up the northwest territory south of the Canadian border, and that's the same country my people are looking at, even though Hudson's Bay already has some posts and Northwest is building some. Most of those are on the Columbia River, we're lookin' to go further inland, and south of the Columbia." He paused, spread his hands, "This country!"

"Have you had many run-ins with the natives?" asked Gabe.

"A few, but mostly we've been peaceful with 'em all. Whenever we come across some new tribe, we hide our guns, at least until we find out if they've ever seen what they call thunder sticks. Don't wanna give 'em any ideas, you know."

"What tribes have you visited?" asked Ezra.

Ross glanced to his partner, frowned a little, then started, "Let's see, the Kalispel, Coeur D'Alene, Spokane, Palus, *Waiilatpus*, Nez Percé, Umatilla," he paused, looked to his partner, "Am I missing any?"

Bertram added, "Okanagan."

Gabe nodded, glanced at Ezra, "Any problems?"

"The *Waiilatpus*, now those people, they control all the peoples around 'em, and they're not friendly with outsiders! I tell you, they are the scourge and terror of all other tribes. We were glad to get out of their country!"

"You're not too far gone from them. They just wiped out a Paiute village not more'n a half a day from here."

The men looked at each other, wide-eyed, and Ross shook his head, "I thought we were done with them."

"Is this the furthest south you've been?" asked Gabe, refilling his cup of coffee.

"Well, ya' see, we been usin' this here map," he reached into his bedroll and withdrew a parchment, "let me show you." Ross lay the map out on the floor of the overhang, placed a couple rocks on the corners, and pointed, "This was made by Peter Pond about ten, twelve year ago, and as you can tell," he pointed to the bottom of the map, "this country is south of what this shows. See there," pointing to a squiggly line that ran east and west, "That's what he shows as the Snake River, and this here is the Snake River plains, but he's a bit off on the river. As you prob'ly know, it runs from the south northward 'fore it turns to the west."

Gabe was fascinated by the map that showed much of the land they had yet to explore. The northern reaches of French Louisiana that included the drainage of the Columbia River. He ran his fingers over the parchment, trying to commit to memory all that he saw about the land they hoped to one day explore. "And you say this is the land of the Kootenai, the Spokane and others?"

"That's right. We been through all that," making a sweeping motion over the upper part of the map, "an' most o' those tribes are right friendly."

Gabe grinned, glanced at Ezra who had come close to examine the parchment as well. "Well, maybe one day we'll have to take a jaunt up that way and see for ourselves!" he declared, sitting back to enjoy his coffee. "So, who were these almighty important men of the Beaver Club that outfitted you for this expedition?" asked Gabe, glancing from Ross to Quigley.

Ross grinned, "Wal, usually I wouldn't say who it was, but I don't see no harm in you youngsters knowin'. Let's see," he glanced to Quigley as he began, "There was Alexander McKenzie, Peter Pond, Simon McTavish, and, uh, oh yeah, John Jacob Astor." He chuckled, "Never could figger out why he used two first names. Most fellas'd just be John or even J.J., but not him, nosiree. Guess ya' gotta have lotsa money to do that."

The conversation continued into the dark of night until all were ready to roll up in their blankets and shed the cool of the night. The fire had faded to grey ashes that hid a few hot coals and gave little heat, but in the wilderness, a fire in the darkness is an invitation to any passersby, four legged and two legged.

13 / PARTING

The morning came quietly, the rains had hushed the cicadas, the owls and the nighthawks, and the morning breeze whisked away the remaining droplets that clung to the tall grass stems and the sage. It was the first light of day that showed a cloudless sky, when the men came from the night's shelter in the overhang.

"Gabe, Ezra, it's been good gettin' to know you gents! Prob'ly won't cross paths again, so, keep your topknot on and ride easy!" declared Ross, his pooched lip and hawk nose belied his friendly temperament, but a light of mischief danced in his narrow eyes. He extended his hand to shake, first with Gabe then Ezra, as his partner, Bertram Quigley followed his action. The men swung aboard, accepted the offered lead for the pack horse from Gabe, then nodded and gigged their horses away. They were bound to the northwest territories and a return to their outfitters in Montreal with their report of the land and the people they discovered.

As they rode away, Ezra said, "And that's how it begins!"

Gabe frowned as he looked at his friend, "What?"

"That's how it begins! They'll take their report back to Montreal, they'll tell about the bounty of furs to be taken and the big money men will outfit an expedition to come down, build forts, trade for furs, and ruin the country. They'll trade with the natives, and ruin the people with their geegaws and doodads, make the natives think they can't live without those things. Then come the settlers, the farmers, the outlaws and . . ."

Gabe chuckled, "Aren't we the soothsayer today! You may be right, but I don't think it's gonna happen very soon. I do believe we've got a few years before this land is overrun with settlers and such."

"Yeah, maybe," resolved Ezra, stepping up on his bay. He waited for Gabe to mount, then the two started to the edge of the flatlands, bound for their postponed get together with Spotted Eagle and his people.

"Have you noticed that here in this wide plain that is perfect buffalo country, we haven't seen any buffalo?" asked Gabe, standing in his stirrups, and looking around to the wide plains that stretched every direction but north.

"Ummhmm, I was hopin' that Spotted Eagle knew

some special place where he was keepin' 'em!" answered Ezra.

Gabe chuckled at the thought of 'keeping' buffalo anywhere. The wooly buggers are bigger than anything else on the prairies and they come and go pretty much as they please. He dropped into his saddle and nudged Ebony on, looking to the northeast for any sign of the Salish. It was late afternoon when they finally spotted the camp at the mouth of a valley that split the long line of timber covered hills. They saw the conical teepees that contrasted with the rolling hills covered with sage and piñon, bunch grass and cacti. As they neared, a contingent of the warriors came toward them boldly, lances and shields held ready for battle, but when one of the men recognized the two riders, he lifted his shield high and shouted, "*ʔe - ʔa!*"

Gabe responded by lifting his hand high and shouting "Hah-Heh!"

The other warriors chattered as they rode near and Gabe recognized the leader of the dog soldiers as Running Wolf, a man they knew from the previous year and their fight with the Blackfoot. Greetings were exchanged and the men rode together into the camp, where many came near to touch and greet the welcome visitors, the children were happy to see Wolf who walked beside Ebony, but allowed children to touch and walk with him. Spotted Eagle came near and spoke, "It is good to see you! We thought maybe you had fallen ill or were taken in battle!"

Gabe chuckled, "And all this time we were worried about you! Did you have a fight with some *Waiilatpus*?"

Spotted Eagle's countenance sobered, and he dropped his eyes, then looked back at his friends, "Yes. They came on us unprovoked. Our scouts had spotted them, there," he pointed to the flats that Gabe and Ezra had crossed, "and we were setting up camp. But I sent several into the trees and when they came, we turned them back. They left with their tails dragging!" He spat the last comment, lifting his head toward the flats as if to send them away.

"Did they do any damage?" asked Ezra.

"One warrior was struck with a spear; one took an arrow. None died, but they lost many! We had the rifles taken from the Blackfoot! They had none! They were surprised when the guns spoke!"

As they talked Spotted Eagle led them to the edge of the camp and a cluster of piñon that sided a small feeder stream with a wide spread of grass. He pointed, "This is a good place for you to camp. Water," pointing at the stream, "grass, and away from the others, like you want."

Gabe grinned, "You know us well, Eagle. Sit a spell, there's something we need to talk about."

Spotted Eagle frowned but sat on a big rock and waited for the two to strip the gear from the horses and rub them down. Small talk was exchanged but as soon as they finished, they sat near Eagle and Gabe began, "Those *Waiilatpus* had just wiped out an entire village of the Paiute before they hit your camp. We came on the site the next morning, buried the dead, and found an old man and a couple young'uns that told us about what happened. We kinda took 'em in, and then the *Waiilatpus* came back, probably after you showed 'em what for, and made camp. Well, you know how it is with us, we don't like seein' young people taken captive and we found out they had some, so. . ."

Before he could continue, Spotted Eagle grinned and interjected, "So you two took the captives back!"

Both Ezra and Gabe chuckled, "You might say that!"

Spotted Eagle frowned, "You must tell me," for he knew by their expression the two friends had more to tell.

Gabe began, but Ezra often added his own comments and told Spotted Eagle about the snakes and the 'Spirit' that danced with the wolf and by the time they were done telling, all three men were laughing and jostling one another at the event that was now quite humorous, but at the time was not. Spotted Eagle said, "Wait until I tell this story at our fire!" referring to the many times the people of the village would gather at the council fire and tell stories of legends, hunts, battles, and more. It was a time of learning, remembering, and sharing and always a special time for the people.

As they tempered their laughter, Gabe grew serious and asked, "Where's the buffalo?"

Eagle also became somber and looked at his friends, "When we scouted them before, the herd was large, covering most of this flat," he motioned to the wide expanse beyond the mouth of the valley. But all the sign shows they have not been here for many days, perhaps since we saw them on the scout."

"But where did they go?" asked Ezra. "They don't migrate south this early in the year, do they?"

"Only if they sense there is an early and hard winter coming. But the signs do not show that."

"So, what do we do now?" asked Gabe.

"We will send out scouts, three or four in each group, three groups, to find the buffalo. If they are to be found and we can make a hunt, we will go after them. If not, then we will return to our village and our families. We will have to hunt for other game to make it through cold season."

Gabe knew the prospects of surviving a long hard winter without ample stores usually provided by their buffalo hunt, would be difficult at best and deadly at worst. It was not a prospect he cared to consider.

Ezra asked, "What about west of here, the land near the place of many waters?"

Eagle nodded, "We have hunted there before, but

this land has always been better. The herds were larger and came every summer. I do not know, but we will do what we can."

"Well, we'll," said Gabe, nodding to Ezra, "be praying about it and maybe we could make a scout for you as well."

Spotted Eagle had grown quiet and when Gabe mentioned praying, he looked up and asked, "Do you pray to the God you told Red Hawk and White Feather about?"

"Yes, we do. We believe He is the God of all, and the Creator of all things."

"Perhaps one day you will tell *me* of this God," suggested Spotted Eagle.

Gabe let a slow smile split his face as he reached his hand to rest on Eagle's shoulder, "I will be glad to tell you about our God, whenever you are ready. Now, if you wish."

Spotted Eagle stood, "I must go to my lodge, my woman waits, and there will be a council before we send the scouts out." He paused, "When you said you would scout, where?"

Gabe stood beside his friend and said, "The Paiute we helped, their village is down by the Snake River, we could go that way and if we see the buffalo before, we'll come back. But if not, perhaps they might know where they will be found."

"That would be good. I will tell the council of this."

14 / PASSAGE

They had an early start and pointed south by southeast. They were moving into a heat scorched land
with sage, browning bunch grass, and cacti and the
cloudless sky promised a dry and hot day of travel.
The creek that came from the valley of the camp,
cut deep across the flats, oftentimes a hundred feet
below the level of the plains, but the ravine provided
protection for both vegetation and the many small
creatures of the plains. Gabe and Ezra crossed the
creek bed when it turned to the southwest and continued on their line of travel, but about a mile after
crossing, a slight rise in the terrain piqued Gabe's
curiosity and he rode straight up the slope before him.
It was a gradual climb and a short distance, but he was
brought to a sudden halt as he came to the edge of a
deep depression. He stood in his stirrups to look into
the huge hole, Ezra doing the same, and they were

surprised to see they were on the edge of a circular shaped hollow about four hundred yards across and about a hundred fifty feet deep. Gabe stepped down, knelt at the edge and looked at what he recognized as a crater, probably made by a striking asteroid. He turned to see Ezra, also on one knee at the edge and gaping at the phenomenon before him.

Ezra looked at Gabe and asked, "What did this?" incredulous at the sight.

"I reckon an asteroid!" as he pointed heavenward.

"And all that rock, from an asteroid?" He motioned to the rock formations that seemed to form a shelf of stone around the upper edge of the hole.

"Well, that I don't know, it looks like that's what's under this dry soil, but I suppose some of it could be from the asteroid," answered Gabe, recalling his studies at the university.

The men stood, looking around at the vast flat that stretched beyond the limits of their vision, and Ezra added, "This is mighty peculiar land, what with them lava fields, this crater, hot springs, and more. Yessir, mighty peculiar!"

"It is that," agreed Gabe as he swung back aboard the big stallion.

They had been watching for any sign of buffalo and had seen some, but pitifully little compared to what they expected and needed to find. A herd of many thousands would leave behind little doubt of their passing, with turned soil, trampled grasses and brush, muddy water holes and dust wallows where the big beasts would roll and cover themselves with dust to ward off bugs. Gabe pointed out, "There's some cowbirds, but not many. They usually follow the herds, but all the sign is several days old."

"And nothing that says a big herd passed this way," added Ezra.

They continued south across the sage brush flat, passing clusters of sage, greasewood and trudging through the dry grasses and rabbitbrush. They kicked out several jackrabbits and Wolf gave chase, caught a couple after a twisting and winding pursuit and ate his fill, coming back to the men with tufts of fur hanging from his jowls and a self-satisfied smirk on his face. But many others dared him to give chase, only to be ignored as Wolf chose to preserve his energy in the rising heat of the day. Even the ever-present rattlesnakes apparently sought some shade, for the mid-day heat would bake them on their preferred flat rock rest stop.

Dust was thick and stifling, no breeze moved the tall grasses and sweat trickled down the backs of the riders as lather colored the chest, inner legs, and the base of the necks of the horses. It was none too soon when the sun lowered to silhouette the distant western mountains and the smell of water and greenery wafted across the path of the travelers. The horses quickened their step and bore a little to the west as the shadowy distance showed green and the slight breeze that came from that way felt cool on the now dry skin of the weary animals and men. As Gabe sat upright, he saw a wide expanse of green that contrasted with the greys and browns they had seen all day, and the setting sun bounced gold and orange off the surface of ponds and bogs. Cattails stood at the far edge, cottonwoods offered recluse and shade, willows waved over the water and waterfowl, ducks, geese, egrets, all enjoyed the unexpected oasis.

The men chose the shelter of the cluster of cottonwood and soon picked their campsite, a site used before by other travelers, proven by the fire ring situated under the long overhanging branches of the tallest cottonwood. They stripped the horses, walked them to the water, let them roll in the grass, then rubbed them down with handfuls of grass. Then they set-to with their own camp. Ezra offered, "How 'bout I start the fire an' such, you take your bow and fetch us some goose to eat?"

Gabe grinned, "I was thinkin' the same thing. It'd be good to have roast goose for a change. I'll see what I can do!" He picked up the leather case with the Mongol bow and his quiver of arrows, sat down and strung the bow, then started toward the marshland at the edge of the watery area. He picked his way through the tall grass that sided the deeper water, careful to test his footing in the boggy bottom, moving slowly and quietly through the watery world. He had spotted some geese with their long black necks and greyish brown feathers, swimming and feeding at the edge of the water and Gabe was slowly working his way to a point with a clear shot. The sun had dropped below the mountains, but the fading light of dusk was enough for Gabe to find his way and see the birds. Within a short while, he was near the edge of the water and parted the tall grasses to see three geese, lazily paddling around, occasionally snatching falling seeds from the surface of the water, as well as diving after some tidbit.

He tied a thin twisted linen string to the arrow, left the remainder looped at his feet, then lifted the bow to take aim. When the chosen goose was broad side, he let the arrow fly, heard the whisper of the soaring missile and the trailing string, then the strike which elicited a squawk and startled the other two that instantly took flight. The targeted bird tried to flutter, but quickly dropped to lie still on the water. Gabe reeled in the long line, bringing the bird to the water's edge and grinned all the while as he withdrew the arrow, wound up the string and replaced the arrow in the quiver.

His return to the camp took only a few minutes and with the big goose dangling at one side, Ezra exclaimed, "Good, good! I was hopin' you'd get one, got everything ready so start pluckin'!"

Gabe grinned, sat down to unstring the bow and

replace it in its case, then went to the willows and started plucking the bird. It was a messy job, but he kept at it, then finished preparing the bird as he dressed it out and returned to the fire for Ezra to take over. Ezra grinned at the bird carcass, still with bits of feather and quills showing, but mostly cleaned. He had prepared a spot for his working and lay the bird down, then stuffed it with camas bulbs, cattail shoots, and onions. He doused it liberally with salt, inside and out, then began plastering it with a thin mud concoction he made up from the nearby water. Once the goose no longer resembled a goose, he walked to a hole he dug near the fire. There was a layer of hot coals in the bottom, crisscrossed with alder sticks, and he lay the goose on the sticks. Then he shoveled more coals in beside the goose, then more alder sticks, more coals, covered it with a layer of sawgrass leaves, then covered it all with a thick layer of dirt. He stepped back, satisfied, looked at Gabe who sat with a quizzical look on his face, then walked to the fire, poured himself a cup of coffee and sat down, stretched out his legs and said, "So, what do you want to talk about?"

"How about where did you get the idea to bury a goose?" asked a flabbergasted Gabe.

"Aww, my momma told me 'bout that, course I never done it before, but I reckon it'll be alright." His thoughts turned to his mother who came from the old country, her heritage of Druids and Celtics had shaped her life and her thinking, as she was known as Black Irish and had many ways about her that were unique and foreign to others. But she taught her son well in all the ways of her people. Although Ezra did not have a university education like Gabe, his education was in many ways just as extensive and useful as was his, even though unconventional. The wisdom and experience gained by each complemented that of the other and the two life-long friends spent their time sharing and teaching one another, either by word or by example.

"So, if it isn't as good as you expect, do we blame you or your mother?" asked Gabe, sipping on his coffee and grinning over the cup.

"If there is any shortcoming to perfection, it would be your fault for your choice of birds, of course!" declared a very stoic Ezra, crossing his outstretched legs at the ankles and lifting his cup to his lips.

Darkness had dropped its curtain over the plains and the stars lit their lanterns as a backdrop to the three-quarter moon that was waxing to full. With the flames dwindled to flickering coals, the camp glowed with the moonlight, long shadows dimpling the flats and the nocturnal creatures began their tune up. Bullfrogs tried to outdo one another, loons startled Gabe, thinking it was wolf howling, but closer. Ezra chuckled, "What's the matter, haven't you heard a loon before?"

"That was a loon? Sounded more like a wolf howling!" The croak of an egret made them turn to look, but the darkness cloaked the entire wetland. Gabe looked at Ezra, "Ain't that goose done yet? I'm hungry!"

Ezra grinned, looked at the night sky and considered the time, guessed about two hours had passed, then said, "I'll check."

With shovel in hand, he began to carefully remove the mounded dirt, then the leaves and green alder branches. He snatched a burning brand from the fire and held it over the hole, smiled and handed the brand to Gabe and worked at removing the goose, now cooked to a deep brown, what he could see of it with the grey ashes and baked mud covering it. He used handfuls of leaves to protect his hands from the heat, and lifted the goose from the hole, sitting it on the rock beside the fire. He dusted off the ashes and baked mud, pulled at the toasted skin, smiled up at Gabe, "It's ready!"

It was quite the delicacy for the men, moist tender meat, crispy skin, and roasted vegetables made a sumptuous feast for the two that had nothing but smoked meat and pemmican for the last few days. They devoured the entire goose, tossing bones and scraps to the bushes for the scavengers, knowing that there would be nothing left come daylight. They turned in with full stomachs, trusting the wolf and the horses to be the guards for the night.

"We will leave, will you join us?" declared Tauitau, speaking to Tawatoy. The two, though rivals, had been friends and foes throughout their childhood and early adulthood. They had gained warrior status together, fought together, hunted together. Though the rivalry was fierce, so was the bond of warriors between the two men.

Tawatoy frowned at Tauitau, "You cannot do this! It will weaken our village; we will be overcome by all our enemies. Even the weak Umatilla that pays us tribute, will no longer pay, and will fight against us as will the Klamath and Palus!"

"But we do not leave our people, we go to take captives, steal horses, and gain honors! We lost face when we came back with our tails between our legs! Pale Eagle's power was gone, and our people paid for that, but now we go to get our power back!" Tauitau spat the words as he leaned toward Tawatoy. "You want to stay with the old men and women, stay! But we go at first light!"

"How many warriors will you take?" asked Tawatoy, fearful for his people.

"Three hands, my brother, Achekaia, and me!" growled Tauitau.

"And do you go against the Salish with their thunder weapons?"

"No! We go against the Paiute! Then if the power is good, we will take the horses and women and more from the Salish, and their thunder weapons will give *us* power!"

The *Waiilatpus*, Palus, Spokane and other tribes of the northern reaches of the Snake River basin had lived in a harsh environment of steep mountains, narrow valleys, tall timber, and rocky hills. The land was not easily accessible by the early French traders and the tribes had not seen the weapons they called thunder weapons. When they were confronted with them in the hands of the Salish, they were astounded and frightened, but when they considered what their enemies had, they knew that same weapon could be great power in their hands.

When the warriors spoke of the weapons, talk quickly turned to how they might attain such power, and it was only Tauitau that offered the possibility of taking them from the Salish. And as in any af-

ter-the-battle talks, much had been said and con-
jectured as to the how and why they could get the
weapons of thunder from their enemies. It was that
talk that drove Tauitau to seize what he saw as an
opportunity to regain his power and status among
the warriors and the warrior societies of the people.

"Then go if you must! I will stay here with the other
warriors and protect our people!" declared Tawatoy,
turning his back and walking away.

They rode into the rising sun when they left their
village on the north flowing Snake River. They knew
it would be a ride of several days, but each day gave
them added resolve to return as great warriors with
many coups, captives, and horses to add to their
wealth and stature within their band. The warriors
were mostly proven, but there were three or four
that had not shed blood in battle, and this would be
the time they prove themselves. They bore names
that told of their youth and inexperience, but if they
were brave in battle, they would be given new names,
names suitable of a proven warrior. Badger, Marmot,
and Squirrel rode together, each one visualizing their
feats in battle. The young men rode at the tail end of
the party that numbered seventeen.

By early mid-day, the third day out, they came upon
a land unlike anything seen by the young men. There
were vast stretches of hot, black lava. With random

flowers and shrubs sprouting through cracks in the hard surface, it appeared as if had been nothing more than a sand painting made by some eccentric shaman, but this surface was hard, hot, immovable. The trail they followed twisted through the maze of strange formations, where rocks were stacked on rocks, lava rose to perpendicular formations that resembled a standing snag of a long dead tree. Other places had holes and undercuts that fashioned caves and tunnels that led to the nethermost regions below. Some vast fields held massive lichen encrusted limestone and granite stones, scattered as if the Creator stood with hands full and flung them at will. Rabbit brush, sage brush, and bitter brush found tenuous footing in the narrow defiles between the big stones and lifted their dull colored branches and leaves to the sun.

"Look!" declared Badger, pointing to a hillside beside the trail. "It looks like folds of buckskin or giant black snakes!" The hillside held ribbons of lava that had flowed from ancient cracks in the earth's surface, eons and even centuries before. They passed a fissure that one of the older warriors, called Black Arrow, said, "That is so deep, you can drop a rock and will not hear it hit bottom!"

The boys looked at one another, eyes wide with wonder as they continued to visually explore the amazing land with its strange formations and configurations. In the distance, steam clouds rose as if they were lazy afternoon clouds that finally rose from their slumbers, but they continued to rise, dissipating as they lifted above the land. It was a barren land that captured and held the heat from the summer sun that forced sweat trails to find release over the backs and necks of the riders that disturbed the silence of the land.

Marmot pointed out a pair of lizards that scampered across a flat lichen covered stone but had to quickly grab at the mane of his horse as it shied away from a sunning rattlesnake. The others laughed at the wide-eyed boy, but he soon had control of his ride and grinned at his friends. Squirrel was the first to spot a bobcat that was on the prowl for his dinner and ignored the passerby, and when Badger pointed out a skunk, everyone gave the striped animal a wide berth.

They were all relieved to leave the land of the lava and see the greenery near the distant Snake River once again. While they traveled almost due east, the Snake River made a wide swooping bend to the south and west, then pointing to the north as it aimed toward the higher mountains and the homeland of the *Waiilatpus* and others. They split two lava fields and were bound for the Snake River, but it was further than they could make on this day.

Random buttes rose out of the flats, a sizable one was easy to see to the south, but smaller ones that rose no more than a thousand feet could be seen in the distance. Tauitau had sent scouts ahead, anticipating their finding the village of the Paiute and perhaps some fresh meat. They were waiting at the base of a smaller butte that showed red and white as it rose about eight hundred feet above the valley floor. Dry grasses, bunch grass, squirreltail, ricegrass and more covered the plains, yet left wide expanses of loose soil and sand that drifted about with the least bit of wind. To the far west, mountains framed the plains while the other points of the compass stood bare yet with low lying clouds that masked any semblance of changing terrain.

It was mid-day after their camp at the butte, that Tauitau led the small band to the bank of the Snake River and allowed the men and horses to drink their fill and even wade into the water for a refreshing swim. The horses were as anxious for the cooling water as were the men and Tauitau stood on the bank with his brother, Achekaia, watching the fierce warriors cavorting like children. He looked at his brother and said, "They do not act like the warriors that will destroy the enemy!"

Achekaia grinned, "When they are rested, they will be all the more anxious for battle!"

"We have much to prove and cannot lose time or warriors," grumbled Tauitau.

"When men are fresh and anxious, they will fight better. You will see."

"But we go against greater numbers! And if we go against the Salish, they have the weapons of thunder!"

"Yes, but that is when you prove yourself as a great leader. When we can take on greater numbers and destroy them, our people will sing songs about you as the leader of a great raid! You will take your place as a chief of our people!"

Tauitau glanced at his brother, pondering his words. Achekaia had long been known as a great thinker and would one day be considered for a chief, but he was not the warrior as his brother. While Tauitau stood just shy of six foot and had broad muscular shoulders and a deep chest, Achekaia was deceptively strong with his lean frame. Yet the younger brother was not just swift of feet, but quick of mind and made wise decisions quickly and easily, while others had to consider the issue. He was also the best tactician of the *Waiilatpus* and had repeatedly proven himself as such.

"We will find the village of the Paiute soon and then we shall see what kind of warriors these may be, but we cannot lose any or we will not go against the Salish," stated Tauitau.

"Then plan wisely, my brother," cautioned Achekaia, pointing with his chin toward the warriors that were coming from the water. "We should go. Perhaps the scouts will bring word of the village."

The Snake River came from the north and the band of *Waiilatpus* followed the river upstream as it wound its way through the thicker vegetation of the lowland. With scouts out ahead and on either side of the river, the band traveled away from the trees, choosing the trail through the taller grasses. There was wheatgrass, bluegrass, and fescue, most standing tall and waving in the late afternoon breeze. They followed a game trail that stayed away from the trees and was probably used more by the antelope and mule deer than natives. As the sun lowered toward the long flat horizon to their left, Tauitau pointed the entourage into the trees to make camp.

They had no sooner started the routine of their camp, gathering firewood to offset the chill of the night, picketing the horses, and laying out their blankets, when the lead scouts rode into camp, broad grins painting their faces. Tauitau and Achekaia came to their sides and nodded for them to tell their findings.

"We found the village of the Paiute! There are many lodges, but many are empty! And there are places where there were lodges but are no more. This is the village of the band we destroyed," reported the first scout.

"How many warriors?" asked Tauitau, frowning at the excitement of the scout.

"We could not tell, but not many," answered the first scout, Red Pony, looking at his fellow scout, Tall Lance.

Lance spoke up, "Perhaps three double hands.

Many are old, some very young."

"How far is the village?" asked Achekaia.

"Half day, maybe less," answered Pony. "The village is on the east side of the river, beyond a sharp bend and where another river joins."

The two leaders, nodded, and turned away to begin their planning for the coming day. But before they attacked, both Achekaia and Tauitau were determined to scout out the village themselves. To attack a well-defended village where the numbers of warriors were greater, they must plan wisely and carefully, for Tauitau's larger plan was to have enough arms and experienced warriors to take on the Salish and capture their weapons of thunder.

16 / PAIUTE

Lone Bear grinned as he watched his grandchildren playing before his lodge. They, Minnow and Antelope, acted as if nothing had happened and that all was right with their world. The older girl, Morning Sun, had gone with the women to gather piñon cones to be roasted for their nuts. Lone Bear remembered the terrible day when the *Waiilatpus* raided the camp of his people that had traveled north for the buffalo hunt, the day when his only son and his woman had been killed, leaving Lone Bear and his woman, Red Deer, to care for the children. He smiled as he thought of his new friends, Spirit Bear and Black Buffalo, the two men who had recaptured his granddaughter, Morning Sun, and her friend, Walks Tall. Although it had only been a few days, the remembered events seemed so long ago.

Lone Bear glanced up to see his woman preparing

food beside the cookfire. He knew she would need firewood, but that was woman's work, but Lone Bear cared little for the prescribed duties between and a man and his woman and had often helped his woman at her tasks as she had helped him. She was better at trapping the salmon in their woven traps, and she could more easily dress and skin any animal that he brought back from his hunts. He also knew she was skilled at the bow and could shoot better than he, so he preferred to not take her with him on his hunts, but occasionally he allowed her to join him, usually on the longer hunts where they would have to stay together in the woods. He grinned at the thought and the memories of many hunts together.

He rose and started to the thick cottonwoods to gather some firewood but was stopped when he saw two of their warriors ride into camp at a gallop, sliding to a stop near the wickiup of the chief, Buffalo Tail. Lone Bear walked closer to see what the men were so anxious about and heard as they excitedly reported, "We saw scouts, scouts of the *Waiilatpus!* There were two, and they talked as they pointed back to our village, then rode off in a hurry!"

Buffalo Tail stood beside the entry to his lodge, frowning at the men, "Where did you see these scouts and how do you know they were *Waiilatpus?*"

Kills Enemy looked at his fellow scout, White Wolf, nodded for him to tell and White Wolf explained,

"One had a buffalo," lifting his hands to his head to resemble the horns of a buffalo, "headdress, and the long fringed leggings. And their horses were different!" The *Waiilatpus* were well-known for their stocky horses that resembled the Morgan horse of the white men and were distinctive from the typical cross-bred lean mustang favored by the plain's tribes.

Buffalo Tail nodded, glanced at a nearby warrior and ordered, "Summon the council!" and turned to go into his wickiup. The dome shaped structure was made with bent saplings and covered with woven brush and sod. The lodge of the chief was larger than most and would accommodate the gathering of the council of elders, the men that the chief would consult about any major decisions that would affect the people. He ducked his head, for he was a tall man, to re-enter his lodge, with but a quick glance back at the others that had gathered.

Lone Bear waited a moment for some of the other elders to come, then ducked into the wickiup with the others, taking their place in the circle of the council. Buffalo Tail looked around the circle, glanced at the two scouts, then began, "Our scouts have told of sighting two scouts from the *Waiilatpus*. He paused a moment, then looked at Kills Enemy, "Tell what you saw."

Kills Enemy and White Wolf were not a part of the council and as such were seated behind the circle.

Standing, Kills Enemy began, "We were scouting and hunting beside the river, downstream about three fingers time. We were stalking some deer near the river; White Wolf was keeping watch from the trees. The deer spooked, ran back from the water to the hills. The scout from our enemy came from the trees beyond the slight hill, crossed the river and joined the other scout. They talked, pointing back the way of our camp, then rode off at a gallop."

"Where did they go?" asked Lone Bear.

Kills Enemy pointed to the south, "We did not follow. We thought it best to return and tell what we saw." He glanced at White Wolf who was nodding his agreement.

The council began to chatter among themselves until Buffalo Tail lifted his hands. When the others grew quiet, he said, "If they are scouting our camp and left quickly to give their report, the raiding party must be close. We must prepare or we will be overrun as were our brothers," he nodded to Lone Bear.

The scouts were dismissed and the elders began talking about what must be done. It was almost an hour before some of the elders filed out of the wickiup, all somber and moving quickly. Lone Bear was one of the last to leave, having been asked by Buffalo Tail to remain and again tell all of those that remained more about the earlier attack. When he explained about the ferocity and vengeful ways of the Waiilatpus, the tribe that would one day be called Cayuse, and how they mutilated the dead, men, women and children, the anger seemed to rise in each of the leaders of the people. Lone Bear glanced from Buffalo Tail, their chief, to Half Face, their war leader, and Spotted Horse, the Puhagim or medicine man, and added, "When our friends, Spirit Bear and Black Buffalo went into their camp and stole our two women back, the Waiilatpus showed nothing but fear and ran away!" He paused, looking from one to the other, "They are a cruel and vicious enemy, but they can be defeated."

The others looked stoically at the old man, then to Buffalo Tail, who responded, "We are grateful for your words. We will make plans as we talked," and dismissed Lone Bear with a nod.

The old man walked proudly from the wickiup of the chief and returned to his own where his woman, Red Deer waited. She had already gathered the necessary firewood and was preparing the fire for the meal, when Morning Sun and Walks Tall returned with two baskets each, all full to overflowing with cones from the piñons. Red Deer smiled, came close to look at the cones, then said, "Now you must gather brush, dry brush, and we will roast the cones so they open, then we can roast the nuts and grind them. They will be good." She smiled at the girls, "You have done well!"

When the girls trotted off to the thickets by the river, Red Deer turned to her man, "What is the council doing?" she demanded.

The old man chuckled, knowing his woman would have nothing kept from her and he explained about the enemy scouts and the planning of the council. "If there is an attack, it will be later tomorrow. They believe the enemy is too far away for an early attack. But our warriors will be ready for them. I believe the leaders will have us," nodding to Red Deer and touching his chest, "and others to be decoys to fool the enemy. We will have our weapons inside the wickiup, but close, so we can use them as we need." Red Deer glared at her man, but she also knew that when an enemy attacks a village, everyone, young, old, men, women, and children are at risk and all must do their part in the fight. She nodded, turned away and went into the lodge, returning with bows and quivers of arrows in hand. She lay them beside her man and said, "Look them over, be sure they are ready." With a quick glance at Lone Bear, Red Deer turned back to her preparations for the meal.

Lone Bear bent to pick up the bow but was startled when the girls came running back, "Grandfather! Grandfather! The men from before, Spirit Bear and the Bonecrusher, they come!"

Lone Bear frowned, looked at Morning Sun, "Bonecrusher?"

"Yes! That is what Walks Tall called him because of how he looks. You remember the story you told us about the legend of the Bonecrusher. What you described was just like him!" pointing to the trees along the bank of the river. The old man grinned, remembering the story of legends that spoke of the spirit man who was darker than others, stronger than all, and would sneak into camps at night and steal girls and boys who had been bad and eat them alive, crushing their bones in his teeth. The old man chuckled at the legend and rose to see if the visitors were indeed the friends they knew.

He walked quickly to the wickiup of the chief to tell him of their visitors, then returned to join the others to see the visitors come near. Four warriors rode out to stop them and now sat their horses, side by side, with war shields and lances held before them. Lone Bear walked forward, wanting to tell the guards that these were friends, and soon neared the four horsemen. He called from behind them, "Kills Enemy!" but there was no response, and he kept walking and called again, "Kills Enemy! These are friends! These are the men that saved our women from the Waiilatpus!"

Kills Enemy turned around to look at the old man, then back at the two strangers that rode closer. The two men each trailed a packhorse and held their free hands high. They held no weapons and came nearer, *"Manahuu!"* called the one with straw colored hair and beard. The other was darker than any man he had ever seen, and Kills Enemy glared at the strange man. The two visitors reined up, rested their hands on the pommels of their saddle and waited. Lone Bear walked between the horses of the guards and continued toward the two men, his hand uplifted and speaking, "Spirit Bear! Black Buffalo! It is good you have come!"

"Lone Bear! Good to see you. We didn't know if this was your village. You look good and we're glad you and the others made a safe journey home."

"Get down, Spirit Bear," he suggested, dropping his eyes to the big wolf that stood between the horses, mouth open and tongue lolling, and if a wolf could have a friendly expression, this one did, but Lone Bear remembered the black wolf and was not alarmed. He extended his hand to clasp the hand of his friend and to Ezra to shake his as well. "Black Buffalo, good friend, welcome."

17 / ALLIES

Lone Bear walked beside his friends and the big wolf as they led the animals into the village. Lone Bear was anxious for the chief and other leaders to meet the two men and talked continually as they made their way to the central compound and the wickiup of the chief. When Ezra noticed the mothers grabbing their children and putting them behind them, his first thought was they were protecting them from the strangers with the big wolf. But he saw some of the children pointing at him and running away, which made him think it was because of his dark color, they had probably never seen a negro before and he grinned at what they might be thinking.

When Lone Bear noticed the reaction of the women and children, he grinned, knowing what it was about and turned to Ezra, "There is a legend, a story that is told, among my people. It tells of one known as Bonecrusher. He is stronger than all men, darker than any, and comes in the night to steal children that have been bad. He eats them alive and crushes their bones with his teeth! One of the girls you rescued told about what they saw and how you terrified the enemies in the darkness. The way she told it, the children thought of Bonecrusher. Now, they think you are the Bonecrusher!" he chuckled as he explained, looking at Black Buffalo as he glanced back at the children.

Ezra looked at Gabe, "Bonecrusher, huh? Sounds mighty fearsome!"

Gabe chuckled, "If they saw you with your war club, they would believe it!"

They came to the central compound where chief Buffalo Tail and the shaman, or Puhagim, Spotted Horse, waited. Gabe saw the two leaders frown at the sight of Wolf and he stifled a grin, trying to stay as stoical as possible. Lone Bear stepped forward and spoke to the two leaders, speaking more rapidly than Gabe could follow, motioning to the two men. He turned to Gabe and Ezra, nodded toward the leaders, "This is the leader of our village, Buffalo Tail, and our Puhagim, what you call a medicine man, Spotted Horse." He turned to the leaders, nodded to the visitors, "This is Spirit Bear and Black Buffalo, the men who took our captive women from the Waiilatpus."

Buffalo Tail stood with a stern expression, glanced to his Puhagim, and looked at the visitors. He kept his arms crossed over his chest but nodded slightly as he looked at each man. There was some chatter between the chief, shaman, and Lone Bear and Lone Bear frowned, then turned to Gabe, "Our chief finds it strange that you would come into our village the same day we spotted scouts from our enemy."

Gabe frowned, "Scouts? From the Waiilatpus?" He looked from Lone Bear to the chief and asked, "Do you expect them to attack your village?"

The chief slowly lifted his head in a nod, still glaring at Gabe as he did, then used sign and the language of the Paiute to ask, "Why do you come at this time?"

Gabe responded with sign and his limited knowledge of the language, "We are on a scout for our friends, the Salish. They came to this valley on a buffalo hunt, but there are no buffalo. We, as have others, are on a scout to find the buffalo. When we saw the smoke from your village, we thought to come see if Lone Bear made his journey home safely."

"The buffalo have moved south early this year. Our people had taken some, but we lost many of our village in the attack by the Waiilatpus. They had gone north after the buffalo."

"Our hearts are heavy for your people. We found the village and buried the dead." Gabe paused a moment, then asked, "If you believe the Waiilatpus are going to attack, if you will allow us, we will fight with you. After what they did, they are our enemy also."

The chief looked sternly at Gabe and Ezra, his brow curling down over his stern eyes. He glanced to Spotted Horse and Lone Bear. He had already noted the weaponry carried by the men and at the thought of their joining the fight, and after the loss of so many of their fighting men, he believed the two visitors would be an asset to the fight. But he was hesitant to say too much to strangers. He nodded slightly, and addressing Lone Bear as much as the visitors, "We will give it much thought. Until then, Lone Bear will show you where you may stay." With another nod, the chief and the Puhagim turned away and ducked into the wickiup.

The village had a combination of brush hut wickiups and teepees, but they were well arranged in the slight valley between two sparsely timbered knolls and back from the thick trees at river's edge. It was well-sheltered, but as Gabe looked it over, he thought it would be hard to defend. They had apparently chosen the camp for shelter rather than defense, and now might pay the price for their choice. As Lone Bear walked them to the edge of the camp near the northernmost knoll, they stopped at the edge of the trees and Lone Bear explained, "What the scouts reported were two of the enemy had seen our village and left hurriedly to return to their raiding party. Buffalo Tail gathered the leaders of the village and the chiefs also worked at a plan to defend the village. You were not a part of that plan and now he must think on what should be done."

"Do you know what the plan might be?" asked Gabe, stripping the gear from the horses, and stacking it near a tall ponderosa.

"They have not told us all, I believe the women and children and some of us old people will stay in the village, to make it look as usual, but with our weapons near. The warriors will probably be placed where they can do the most, but how, I do not know," answered Lone Bear.

Gabe stopped what he was doing and stood, hands on hips, and looked around the village and terrain. Behind the camp, the valley narrowed and was thick with trees and undergrowth that would probably hinder if not prohibit any attackers coming down the valley. Two low knolls, standing maybe two hundred feet, at their highest, above the camp and had considerable timber, but more sparse than the trees and shrubs that lined the river bank. Along the river, on both sides, were oft used trails that were widened by travois and hunting parties and would be the obvious route of attack, but an enemy that were known for their war-like ways would not be easily predictable.

Gabe looked at Lone Bear, "Black Buffalo, or Bonecrusher," he chuckled at the reference, "and I will take a look around. It would probably be best, if Buffalo Tail is willing for us to be involved, if we were allowed to fight when and where we could do the best, moving about and attacking as we can."

"I will talk with Buffalo Tail. I believe he would think that best as well."

After Lone Bear left and the two friends had fashioned their camp, suitable for the short stay, Gabe turned to Ezra, "Let's take a look around, see what might be comin' our way."

"That's the best idea I heard all day. I don't like just waitin' on somebody to bring the fight to me, I'd rather do the choosin' my own self!" declared Ezra, snatching up his rifle and checking the load and priming as they started into the scattered trees, to mount the taller of the two knolls. Gabe was one that always sought the high ground, and this high ground was not high enough to suit him, but they would have to make the most of what they had. Once they crested the knoll, they found a bald knob, with a sizable stack of lichen covered limestone boulders, a snag of a piñon growing from a crack and scattered scrub oak brush about. The promontory offered a good view of the far side of the river and the trail leading to the south. The knoll south of the village was similar, the top easily seen from this larger butte. The trees that dappled the hillside were mostly piñon, none standing over ten feet tall and well scattered on the slope. Gabe carefully examined the view of the village and the trail beyond, thinking as a shooter.

Most of the village would be well within the range of his Ferguson, but the far perimeter near the river was a little beyond accurate shooting range. He usually calculated two hundred yards to be the far reaches of his Ferguson. However, he was known to use his Mongol bow and score a hit on a man-sized target at about four hundred yards, but he didn't want to bet his life on it. Ezra could take down a target at two hundred yards with his long-barreled Lancaster rifle, but he preferred the close in combat with his war club and tomahawk.

Gabe looked at his friend, "What do you think?"

Ezra had been searching the trees and the terrain and was so focused on what he was considering, he was startled by Gabe's question, but turned and answered, "I'm thinkin' they'll either try to come over that knob yonder, depending on what the trail looks like on the other side, or come from the trail or cross the river. But if they cross the river, I figger they'll do it upstream, yonder, then come at the village down thisaway," he pointed toward the river bank and the edge of the butte that pushed the river away to make a 'u' shaped bend. "Or, maybe both, split their forces and come from both ways."

Gabe nodded, then pointed across the river, "And see that butte yonder, that'd be a good place for their war leader to direct the battle. They can prob'ly see right into the village, through that break in the trees by the bank."

"Ummhmm," agreed Ezra. "Let's go take a look from that knob yonder," pointing across the village to the far butte.

They started off the hillock and worked their way through the piñon and juniper, Wolf between the two, and bottomed out, then started across the flat behind most of the village. They had passed several lodges, drew some curious stares, until Morning Sun and Walks Tall came running toward them. Both girls were laughing and smiling and waving as they neared then greeted the men with hugs. They stepped back and started chattering, but Gabe lifted his hand, "Whoa, slow down," he spoke with sign and his limited Paiute, which was similar to Shoshone which he understood. When the girls started again, Morning Sun spoke and Walks Tall signed, and Gabe and Ezra were able to make out most of what was said, as long as their excitement did not override their words.

"We are so glad you came! Our friends would not believe us when we told them about being taken and how you rescued us," both girls looked at Ezra, laughing, "and no one believed we knew you!"

Gabe motioned for them to follow as they continued toward the other butte, and Ezra answered, "You mean Bonecrusher?"

The girls stopped, looking at Ezra wide-eyed,

and Morning Sun spoke softly, "You are not Bone-crusher, are you?"

Ezra grinned, kept walking and laughing, said, "I didn't even know who he was until Lone Bear told us. All I did the night we took you back was dance and shout with Wolf here, it was the paint that Spirit Bear put on me and the rest of it that scared those warriors away."

The girls laughed and Morning Sun asked, "Where are you going?"

"Oh, just up the butte here, to look around a little," explained Gabe, choosing not to reveal the danger that might be coming if the Waiilatpus were to attack. Once atop the crest, they made careful observations, pointing out the trail, the camp, and the trees at the river. They spoke almost in riddles, as they suggested different approaches and trails and more, wanting to keep their thoughts from the girls and not alarm them unnecessarily.

Morning Sun said, "Grandmother told me you were to come to our lodge to eat with us."

Gabe glanced at Ezra, who let a smile split his face, then turned to Morning Sun, "Your grandmother is the wife of Lone Bear?"

"Yes. And Walks Tall will be there too!" nodding to her friend.

"Then you tell your grandmother we will be glad to come," answered Gabe.

The girls were excited and trotted off, slipping and sliding down the gravelly trail to the bottom of the butte, then took off at a run toward the lodge of Lone Bear. Gabe and Ezra chuckled as they watched the girls leave, then Ezra said, "We can't let anything happen to those two, not after what they've already been through."

"Ummhmm," answered Gabe, taking another quick glance around, "You satisfied with what you see here?" The top of this knoll was similar to the other, with big boulders, scrubby piñon, some bunch grass and cactus. The view of the trail was spotty, but sufficient and the cover on top was good. Neither man planned on spending the entire battle atop the buttes, but would use the promontory to observe, maybe some shooting, but most would happen below. Mainly, they wanted to prevent any of the Waiilatpus from gaining the high ground and using it against the villagers.

They descended the butte by the zigzag trail that wound through the trees and brought them into the edge of the village. They would check on their horses and gear before going to the lodge of Lone Bear, but Ezra's stomach was already growling with hunger and he would allow no delays.

18 / TACTICS

The typical native village comes to life before first light. Women are stoking up fires, men are traipsing to the woods, and children are stretching and cavorting by the dim light of early morning. Gabe and Ezra had saddled their horses, taking all their weapons, and started to the hilltops for their usual morning time with the Lord. In addition to their weapons, they had the 'Sword of the Spirit' in the scriptures to arm themselves for the day.

As Gabe crested the north butte, he dismounted, loosened the girth on Ebony and tethered him below the crest in a small cluster of piñon with bunch grass nearby. With rifle in hand and the case with the Mongol bow and both saddle pistols tucked in his sash with the Bailes over/under pistol, the quiver of arrows hung from his belt, he was loaded and primed for the day. Wolf trotted to the limestone boulders,

found a flat rock and stretched out to enjoy the cool
of the stone, and watched as Gabe situated himself on
the promontory. Gabe used the cover of the scraggly
piñon to shield himself from the view of anyone below, then sat down to string the bow. With weapons
in place and ready, he faced the edge of the camp
where he could see any movement on the trail that
followed the river to the north, opened his Bible and
sat cross-legged to enjoy the warmth of the rising sun
on his back.

Ezra had done much the same as he nudged his
bay near the crest of the south butte, picketed him
and with rifle in his left hand, his gun-stock shaped
ironwood war club in the other, and his pistol, tomahawk, and knife in the sash, he maneuvered his way
to the rocky top of the butte to his chosen point on
the crest. This butte had a few more scrub oak and
piñon than the north butte where Gabe was, but the
cover was good and the line of sight excellent. He was
to watch the trail from the south that paralleled the
river and the flat beyond the river, for any unusual
activity. Once situated and comfortable, choosing a
flat stone with a larger one behind it for a back rest,
he stretched out his legs and gave the area a once-over
by the dim early light. Satisfied, he pulled out his Bible
and started his morning routine.

When Buffalo Tail, Spotted Horse, Half Face, and
Lone Bear came to their camp the previous night,

they discussed what ways the two visitors could be helpful in the anticipated fight with their enemy, the Waiilatpus. "Well, chief," began Gabe, "when we hit their camp in the night, Black Buffalo there was painted up like a skeleton ghost, and he screamed and hollered as he danced with Wolf there. That scared the wits outta them warriors and they up jumped and ran like they was snake-bit, 'course some of 'em were cuz we threw some rattlesnakes among 'em also."

The Paiute leaders laughed at the image, an image even Lone Bear had not seen, and Gabe continued, "But we can't do that durin' the day. But we've got some rifles and such that might give us an advantage."

"We have only two warriors that have rifles, but they do not do much more than smoke and make noise. They traded three horses, six pelts, and more for them," explained Lone Bear, shaking his head. "They were foolish," he concluded.

"Well, we can do more than make smoke with 'em," explained Ezra.

Gabe nodded, then added, "We took a walk up on the buttes," nodding toward the two buttes, "to have a look-see, and that might be a good place for us to start out."

The chief agreed, "We know that must be protected to keep the enemy from attacking from there. We lost many of our warriors and there are many places to protect." He paused, dropped his head and looked back at Gabe, "Our plan was to have the old men and women stay in camp, to make it look natural, then once the attack begins, have our men come from the trees to strike from behind," he paused, then added, "We do not expect them until about mid-day, but we will prepare early."

"That is a good plan chief, and if we," nodding to Ezra, "are up high, we can see them coming and give a warning. And we can keep them from taking the hilltops to attack from above."

"What warning would you give?" asked Half Face, the war leader, frowning and repeatedly glancing at Wolf as he lay beside Gabe. The war leader was an intimidating warrior, having earned his name by his visage that bore a jagged scar that ran from above his left ear across and down his cheek to the point of his chin, giving his mouth a downward turn on that side and his left eyelid never closed completely.

Gabe grinned, reached into his possibles pouch and withdrew a highly polished disc that was used as a mirror. He used the brightness of the fire and reflected the light into the eyes of the Puhagim. "We use these to signal one another, and we can signal you or your men wherever they are, as long as we can see them. That way, there's nothing to warn the enemy they have been spotted."

The medicine man looked to the chief and war leader, and slowly nodded, maintaining his somber expression. The chief explained where he and the war leader would be, then extended his arm to affirm the plan. Gabe reached forward, clasped forearms with the chief and shook, nodding as he did, glancing to Ezra. The four visitors rose, the war leader giving a glance back at the wolf, and walked into the darkness.

Gabe was comfortable, but that premonition of prickly skin at his back and neck gave a subtle warning. He rocked his shoulders back as he lifted his eyes to search the area before him. He had given considerable thought to the possibilities of the attack and how *he* would plan such an assault. For the attack to come from the north, they would have to either circumvent the camp through the hills behind him, or cross the flats beyond the river to get upstream and come to the trail, for they were known to be south of the camp. But for them to get upstream, they would have to make that move in the night to prevent being seen and warn the village. He took a deep breath as he looked around, closing his Bible and setting it aside as he looked. He glanced down to see Wolf lying contentedly and with his face between his paws, undisturbed.

Again that feeling of unease seemed to make his heart skip a beat. He glanced to the far butte, saw nothing from Ezra, then reached down at his feet and slipped the brass telescope from its case. With a quick look behind him to the rolling flats and hills beyond, he lifted the scope to search the northern brush and trees at river's edge. The sun was stretching its golden lances from below the eastern mountains and the sky illumined with hints of gold. The low light was enough for Gabe to search the area, but he saw nothing but some mule deer tiptoeing to the river for their morning drink. He slowly brought the scope along the line, moving back and forth to take in every bit of brush and scrub trees that could provide cover. He paused, moved the scope back to the thicker trees and a slight draw that led to the river.

He held the scope in place, waiting, and was rewarded by the swishing of a horse's tail. Enough to tell him they had picketed their horses in the draw and were approaching on foot. He searched the trail, gullies, brush and more and finally spotted the moccasined foot of a single warrior that lay behind a clump of sage. Then focusing on that area which was about a hundred yards from the point of the knoll and spotted a couple more. He lowered the scope, gave a quick overview of the area and probable approach of the warriors, and knew they would possibly try to climb the mount where he sat to approach the village from the high ground.

He grabbed his mirror, flashed Ezra, received an answer, then gave two flashes to indicate there were as many as ten warriors on his side. Then Gabe turned to signal the chief and war leader where they lay hidden in the brush at the edge of the river and the village. Once the warning was given, he replaced the mirror and picked up his bow. If he could take out a warrior or two without giving away his position and that they were seen, it would be to their advantage.

He nocked an arrow, waited a moment, and chose the warrior that lay behind the sage. He brought the bow to full draw, sighted in on the target that lay about a hundred twenty yards, downhill, and in the brush. With a slight elevation as he sighted, he let the arrow fly. He watched the arrow in flight as he unconsciously lifted another arrow from the quiver and nocked it, just as the first arrow found its mark. He saw the kick of the foot but heard nothing and the moccasined foot did not move again. The fletching of the arrow could be seen only because of the contrasting color of the dark feather in the blue grey shrubbery.

Gabe, staying partially obscured beside the scraggly piñon, searched for another target. As he watched, he saw two warriors rise and staying in a low crouch, rush to another brush or tree, and he waited. Another warrior revealed his position as he slowly rose, and started to move as did the others, but Gabe's arrow whispered through the morning air and buried itself in the man's chest, causing him to fall backward. His movement and cry of alarm, gave warning to the others and within moments, several warriors rose from cover and started their charge. Gabe watched as three started around the point and two started to climb the knoll where Gabe waited. He was well hidden, and the attackers were not sure where the arrow came from, looking at nearby trees and cover with no thought given to the hilltop, for in their minds, no one could possibly shoot an arrow from that distance with any accuracy. And Gabe waited. He touched the handle of his Bailes pistol but would use the bow first.

He was facing north, away from the camp, and was a little surprised to hear the blast of Ezra's Lancaster rifle and knew the rest of the enemy were attacking from the south as expected. Gabe caught sight of the first warrior as he paused behind a piñon, probably to catch his breath and possibly having heard the report of the rifle. The second warrior broke from cover and was rewarded with a long black arrow that pierced his chest, driving him off his feet to fall with his head downhill and gasping for his last breath. The man behind the tree was closer to Gabe when the arrow took the other and he charged up the hill, even though he had not seen Gabe.

Gabe dropped the bow, slipped the tomahawk from his belt and waited. Wolf let a low growl come from his deep chest, but Gabe spoke softly and told the beast to stay. The warrior paused as he reached the boulders, searching for a point to look down at the camp and Gabe stepped from behind the rocks and scraggly tree, within arm's length of the man. His foot dislodged a small stone that rattled and gave the warrior warning. The man held a bow with an arrow nocked, and turned to face the attack, but was an instant too slow as the war hawk struck him just above his left eye, splitting his skull and dropping him on his face. Gabe stepped back to let the man fall, wiped his tomahawk on the man's leggings, replaced it in his belt and returned to his promontory to retrieve his rifle and bow. As he lifted the Ferguson, he saw the attack at the edge of the village, saw a charging Waiilatpus warrior and quickly lifted the rifle, earing back the hammer as he did. With a quick sight, on the charging warrior, he squeezed off his shot and the big rifle bucked and boomed, belching a cloud of smoke and sending the deadly ball on its way. The targeted warrior was stopped by the impact that took him high on his chest at the base of his throat and blasted a massive hole as it exited his back, taking with it a portion of his spine. The man fell backwards, wide eyes staring at the sky that now showed a pale blue.

Gabe heard a piercing scream of a war cry that he recognized as Ezra's and swung his head to look at the far butte. Atop the knoll, he saw Ezra, shirtless, and standing in a wide stance, swinging his war club two-handed and with the first swing, beheaded a charging warrior. The halberd blade which Ezra kept as sharp as his knife, carried the head off and sent it rolling toward another charging warrior that paused in his charge to see the head of his friend tumbling down the hillside like a ripe fruit that fell from a tree.

Ezra shouted his war cry, swinging the war club overhead, as another warrior dared approach, the man had an arrow nocked and lifted his bow, but before he could bring it to full draw, Ezra snatched his pistol from his belt, and let it blast. The big lead ball caught the warrior at the base of his sternum and bent the man in half as it ripped through his body. The warrior's arrow flew wide, trembling like a hawk with a broken wing, and fell harmlessly beside the lone tree near the crest of the hill. The third warrior saw the second kill of the crazed man with the dark skin, and with another glance at his friends, turned and ran down the butte, slipping and sliding and glancing back to make sure he wasn't followed.

Ezra looked down the slope, saw the man running and that there were no more coming, then turned to look across the way to the butte where Gabe stood. The men lifted their hands for a quick wave, then gathered their weapons and went to the horses to rejoin the battle that waged below.

19 / BATTLE

As Gabe turned to start back to where Ebony was tethered, something caught his eye and he paused, then looked across the river to the tall butte beyond. Atop the butte at a point where most of the village could be seen, were two men on horseback. One had a typical halo style war bonnet, the other showed long braids, and a topknot with two or three feathers. They were obviously the leaders of the raiding party, watching the battle from the butte, directing the attack from afar. Gabe stared for just a moment, glanced to the village, then hurried to mount up and go to the fight.

Gabe had reloaded the rifle and now mounted, he checked the loads and priming on both saddle pistols, and his belt pistol. The Mongol bow was safely stashed in its case that hung beneath the left fender leather of the saddle, the quiver hung on the right tie down behind the cantle, but he held the rifle across the pommel, thumb on the hammer, ready to lift and fire as needed. He gigged Ebony to take the trail off the butte that led to their camp at the east edge of the village, then stormed into the fight. He spotted an enemy warrior dragging a young woman, his hand twisted in her hair, a tomahawk in his free hand lifted high as he screamed his triumphant war cry. Without pausing a step, Gabe lifted the Ferguson, fired it like a pistol, winced at the pain in his wrist, but never lost his grip. As he slid the rifle into the scabbard under his right leg, he saw the screaming warrior stumble and fall, having dropped his warhawk and grabbed at his side where the big lead ball started tearing its way crosswise through his body, to blow a fist sized hole under his left arm, breaking the arm as it exited. The girl grabbed at his hand, tore it free from her hair and stood to run back to her lodge. Gabe grabbed a saddle pistol as he reined Ebony among the lodges, saw a Waiilatpus warrior lift his knife high as he straddled an old man, and swung the pistol to bear, pulled the trigger and felt the pistol buck as it expelled the bullet in a cloud of smoke. The bullet flew true and exploded the warrior's head when it shattered his jaw bone and blasted out the other side. Gabe cocked the second hammer on the double-barreled pistol, and let Ebony pick his way among the lodges, following Wolf as the beast stalked his way among the pandemonium.

Gabe glanced to the edge of the village and saw Ezra aboard his big bay. Ezra charged into a group of attackers, swinging his war club both right and left, guiding his horse with his knees. He crowded between two young warriors who turned to see the fearful black fighter, just before they felt the crushing blow of the war club. Ezra swung the club in a swooping circle parallel to his mount, the big ball that held the halberd blade striking the skull of the warrior, crushing it and dropping him instantly in a heap. Without the slightest hesitation in his oft-practiced swing, Ezra brought the war club in a similar loop on his off side, and clubbed down the second warrior. He looked up to see two warriors frantically taking flight from the battle, crashing through the trees and diving into the river.

Ezra reined up, looked about and saw no targets. Several of the Paiute warriors and a couple grey haired men came running from the village, searching for any enemies, but there were none. He saw Gabe leaning over the neck of Ebony, stroking the big black and talking to him as they came toward Ezra. The two men sat up, grinned at one another, then looked at the village warriors as they crowded into the trees at the bank of the river. They stood, waving their weapons, and shouting as they saw the two fleeing warriors climb from the water on the far side. More insults were shouted, but the cacophony soon died down and the relieved warriors came from the river to return to the village.

Buffalo Tail walked beside Half Face as the two men approached Gabe and Ezra, sitting on their horses, and talking. Gabe looked up, saw them approaching and spoke softly to Ezra. "Here they come. Wonder how they did?"

Buffalo Tail stopped before the men, frowning, looked at Ezra with his shirtless torso and sweat dripping and said, "Half Face killed one, another was wounded but fled, and we saw the two at the river. But where are the others? Did they dare attack a village with so few?"

Gabe fidgeted a little in his seat and glanced at Ezra, then back at the chief, "I reckon you'll find a couple on the butte yonder," pointing with his chin to the south butte where Ezra had battled, "And maybe a few more on that'n," pointing with a nod to the north butte. "Maybe a couple others in the brush." He paused, "Might be a couple back there," nodding toward the east end of the village." He dropped his gaze to look at Wolf who had dropped to his belly beside Ebony, then looked back to the chief, "The two leaders were on the butte yonder, watching from a distance. But I reckon they high-tailed it outta here when they saw their men had failed."

Gabe glanced at Ezra, "Oh yeah," and twisted in his saddle, "I think Bonecrusher here done in a couple more back there," he pointed behind them at the two bodies crumpled beside the trail. Lone Bear had come near and looked at his two friends, "My woman says she will have food ready soon, if you will join us."

Ezra grinned and answered, "Yes indeedy! I just need to clean up and take our horses back to camp and we'll be right along! I kinda worked up an appetite!"

They nodded to the chief and war leader, then reined their mounts around to return to their camp. Lone Bear, Buffalo Tail and Half Face stared at their backs as they rode through the village to their camp. Buffalo Tail turned to Half Face, "Go, look for the bodies of those there," pointing to the north butte, "and beyond. There should be horses or sign of more warriors." He turned to Lone Bear, then spotted a young warrior and motioned him over. Looking at the young man, he said, "Black Fox, go to that butte, look for bodies and horses. Return to tell me what you find." The chief watched the young man leave, then turned again to Lone Bear, "Look at those two, see how they were killed and take what they have," motioning to the two dead beside the trail. He shook his head as he watched the old man walk up the trail, then started for his wickiup. He was struggling with what had happened, how so few were killed by his people, none of his people were killed although three were wounded. He was puzzled over the events and would have to wait until he heard from the others.

***

What had seemed like hours, had taken just a handful of minutes and it was over. What they had thought would be a quick and easy victory with an abundance of bounty and blood honors for the warriors of the Liksiyu, or as others called them, the *Waiilatpus*, had suddenly become a rout, and most of the warriors were dead or wounded. Achekaia looked at his brother, Tauitau, shook his head and nudged his horse to the trail that would take them off the butte. The men had been determined to scout out the village before the attack, but the report of the scouts said the village had nothing but old people and women and children. They assumed the warriors were gone on a buffalo hunt and were certain the village would be an easy victory. Tauitau said their scout was unnecessary if they rode through the night and attacked the village early before any warriors could return.

When they stopped beside the two warriors that came from the river, Tauitau barked, "What happened? Why did you run?"

The young man, Badger, dropped his eyes and hung his head. The other warrior, Tall Lance, who was bleeding from a wound on his thigh, looked defiantly at the leader and his brother and spat, "There were those with thunder weapons! And the black spirit from the raid against the other village, the one that danced with the Black Wolf and threw the snakes among us, he was there and danced with his war club, killing everyone! He cut the head off Black Arrow!"

Tauitau turned on his brother, "I said I saw the black spirit!"

"That was no spirit! That was a man with dark skin, I have heard of them, and they are great warriors, but not a spirit!" spat Achekaia. "You have no power! You are no different than the shaman, Pale Eagle, the man you killed! You will have no power until you make that right!"

Achekaia said to the two warriors, "Get your horses, the horses of the dead, and we will return to our village!" He jerked the head of his horse around, faced his brother, "Will you return with us?" he snarled.

"I will go after those two that have the thunder weapons! I will take their power and then I will return!" barked Tauitau. He returned to the trail at the base of the butte. He was determined to see the strange men with the thunder weapons and see if the one was a black spirit or not. He tethered his mount at a juniper cluster, and with bow in hand, started up the trail at the back side of the butte. If he were careful, he could observe the village and any activity from the crest of the butte, and not be seen. If the two men with the thunder weapons were in the camp, or if they left, he would know and would follow or if they stayed, he would take them in the night. Tauitau was known for his stealth and his deadly work in the darkness.

20 / RETURN

The battle was over and life resumed as normal in the village of the Paiute. In the days before the attack, most of the women had been involved in the gathering of the annual piñon nut harvest and now fires blossomed throughout the village to bake and roast the nuts. The women stacked the piñon cones in tall piles, covered the stack with dry brush and set the brush afire. The flames burnt off the pine sap, and the heat opened the cones to drop the rich nuts in a heap. Once the flames subsided, the women checked each cone, removed the remaining nuts and the harvested nuts with the thin shells were roasted, dried, and ground into a flour for breadmaking and more.

Morning Sun and Walks Tall heard that the visitors were leaving soon and together with another young woman, Prairie Rabbit, the girl being drug by her hair by an attacker and saved by Gabe, they wanted to show their appreciation. The three came to the lodge and cookfire of Lone Bear, and Morning Sun spoke, "Grandfather, Spirit Bear, we are grateful for all you have done for our people and we wanted to show our thanks. We have so little and cannot give what we would like, but we worked hard for this," she nodded at the parfleche. "We show you we are grateful by offering you this parfleche with piñon nuts. We know you have women who will use these for their family. You would honor us if you would accept this gift." Morning Sun stepped back from the parfleche, head down and stood beside the other girls.

Gabe glanced at Ezra and Lone Bear, then to the girls. He stood and walked to the parfleche, dropped to one knee, and opened the flap on the rawhide container. It was filled to the brim with roasted piñon nuts, he guessed there were probably twenty to twenty-five pounds of nuts. It was a special gift and would have required considerable time and work by the girls to amass the bounty. Gabe smiled, looked at the girls, "We are honored to accept. Our wives," nodding to Ezra, "will be very grateful for this gift."

"And we will too, especially when they make bread with them!" declared Ezra, grinning broadly. The girls smiled and nodded then turned away and quickly left, the usual embarrassment of young girls showing by their expressions and giggles.

Red Deer stood beside the hanging pot at the fire,

looked at the men and said, "What they give you is several days of their lives. To gather that many," nodding to the parfleche, "would take one woman," then held up one hand, all fingers extended, "this many days just to get them. Then one day to roast and pick them. It is hard work and a special gift."

Gabe glanced at Ezra, "We have not been in places where the piñon are plentiful, but we know how hard they are to gather. We are grateful for the gift and our wives will be also."

Red Deer huffed, then bent to her work as the men had finished the meal and stacked the wood troughs and utensils beside the fire. Lone Bear stood to join them as they walked to their camp to prepare to leave, "It has been good for you to be here. Buffalo Tail knows you saved many lives of the Numu and we will always be grateful. You will always be welcome in our village."

"Thanks Lone Bear. We're glad you and the young'uns are alright. But we may come back someday, bring our women and youngsters."

"That would be good." He stepped back as Gabe and Ezra swung aboard their mounts and waved as they rode out of camp. They crossed the river and took to the same trail to return to the camp of the Salish, knowing the ride would take at least a day and a half, and they planned on camping near the place with many ponds, bogs, and tall grasses. Ezra offered,

"Since we had goose last time we came through here, whatcha think about sumpin' different?"

"Like what?" responded Gabe.

"Oh, fish, might find some brookies in one o' them ponds."

"So, what you're really sayin' is you want to do the fishin' while I do the cookin'.'"

"Sounds 'bout right, since I'm a better fisherman anyway."

They left the grasslands and were crossing the wide expanse of sage flats. The sage and greasewood were thick and tall, and the trail twisted through the thickets. Ezra saw Gabe rolling his shoulders and looking around and asked, "What? What is it?"

"Somethin's wrong," answered Gabe, reining up and standing in his stirrups to look about. The sage was knee high as they straddled the horses and could easily hide any number of dangers. But nothing showed, yet Gabe was uneasy. He reached back to slip the scope from the saddle bags, extended it, and began to scan their surroundings. As he sat, one foot in a stirrup, the other leg across the seat of the saddle and he looked at the trail they had just traveled. He stood motionless, watching. "Somebody's followin' us. Can't make 'em out, looks like just one."

"Somebody from the village?"

"Don't think so, don't appear to be in a hurry to catch up."

Gabe sat back in the saddle, replaced the scope, "Guess we'll just have to wait 'n see."

When the sun was cradled in the western peaks, the gold of late afternoon bouncing off the ponds of the marshland, and Ezra was complaining about being hungry, Gabe nodded to the north, "There's a little knoll yonder, 'pears to be the highest point around. You go ahead and make camp, take the pack horse here and I'm goin' up there to see if I can get a better look at whoever that is followin' us."

Ezra dropped his gaze then looked back at his friend, "Yeah, I've been feelin' it too. Ain't nothin' good about it neither." The men had learned to pay attention to Ezra's premonitions and Gabe nodded, looking a little squint-eyed at his friend and said, "Watchur back."

"You too."

They parted ways and Ezra took to the tall grass, showing little sign of his passing, but Gabe stayed on the dry land at the edge of the grass, intentionally leaving clear tracks of his direction. If the follower was close behind, he wanted to draw him closer and make a better target of the man, if he proved to be an enemy.

The bit of a knoll rose no more than fifty or sixty feet above the valley floor, but with the flat land and rolling terrain, it was the best point for any observation. Gabe tethered Ebony to a tall sage, and with

Wolf at his heels, he climbed the crescent shaped knoll. Once atop, he dropped to one knee, extended the scope and quickly looked at their backtrail. But the distance from the knoll to the sage lowland was no more than three miles and the marshland lay at the foot of the knoll. If anyone was purposefully following, they would probably be smart enough to not show themselves and stay in the cover of the tall sage.

Nothing moved, save a couple jackrabbits trying to outsmart a skinny coyote. Gabe allowed his attention to be taken by the wildlife footrace, but only for a minute. Then looked back at the edge of the sage just in time to catch a glimpse of the follower. He stopped at the last sage clump and was slipping from his horse, when Gabe saw the movement. The man was bare chested, wore leggings and a breechcloth, long black braids, and feathers in a topknot. Yet all Gabe could distinguish was the man was Indian, there was nothing significant in what he saw that would tell of his people, and certainly nothing that would explain his following them.

Gabe bellied down beside Wolf, looked at his furry friend and said, "Well, boy. Looks like we might be waitin' a while. Dunno who that varmint is, but I don't like it none." He lifted the scope again, glanced at the sun and the position of his scope, then grabbed a piece of buckskin from his possibles pouch and draped it over the end to keep the setting sun from bouncing some light off the lens and warning the follower. The hood shaded the lens and Gabe looked again, but there was nothing showing the man had ever been there. Gabe moved the scope over the expanse of the sage, returning again and again to the last spot where he saw the man, but nothing showed.

He chuckled and said to Wolf, "He musta heard us, boy. He prob'ly found him a hidey hole in that sage yonder and will likely wait 'till dark 'fore he tries anything. Guess we'll just hafta be ready for him, ya' reckon?" He crabbed back from the crest, rose and strode down the back slope and hurriedly mounted Ebony and took to the marshland.

Ezra had stripped the pack animals, tethered his bay, and disappeared into the greenery of the marshland, looking for a fishing hole. Gabe chuckled, stepped off his horse, stripped off the gear and rubbed him down with a handful of dry grass. Then with a long tether, he rubbed the black's neck and said, "Enjoy the grass boy," and went to the fire ring to arrange the already gathered firewood to start a small cookfire. He glanced up at the hemlock that overshadowed the ring and was pleased with the overhanging branches that would dissipate the smoke. He brought out his flint and steel, struck sparks onto the fluff from a dead cattail, saw smoke and blew lightly, then moved the fluff to the tinder, a few more puffs on the smoldering spark and a little flame leaped up, catching the tinder. Gabe sat back, slowly feeding the tinder a few sticks and the fire soon flared. He fanned the flames a little, moved the sticks apart to make a flatter fire, and picked up the coffee pot to fetch some water for their favorite brew.

Within moments, the coffee pot was dancing on the flat rock and the frying pan had the grease sizzling, and Ezra pushed through the currant bushes, smiling broadly with a forked branch bearing several fat brook trout. After rolling them in the cornmeal, Ezra lay them in the sizzling grease and pushed the frying pan closer to the flames. He glanced at Gabe, "So, you see anything?"

"Got a glimpse of him, just before he dropped back in the sage and lay low. All I could tell was he was an Indian, big fella, but what people, I dunno."

"Hmmm, so you reckon he'll hang back till dark?"

"I'm thinkin' that's his plan. I don't think he saw me on the knoll but might have after I came down. Might just be somebody that saw us with packhorses and figgered we might have somethin' he wanted."

"Well, for right now, I'm for eatin'!" declared the always hungry Ezra, grabbing up his plate and cup.

Gabe grinned, "No sense dying on an empty stomach!"

21 / TAUITAU

Tauitau was a patient man, up to a point. When he was focused on vengeance, the bitterness of defeat ate at him as he lay belly down on the top of the butte beside the Snake River. He watched the village of the Paiute, saw the people gather the bodies of the warriors that had followed him and his brother, Achekaia, in hopes of gaining honors and plunder. Some had hoped to capture a woman or two to take back to the village and make them slaves. Others had dreams of adding to their wealth by taking many horses, the standard by which the Liksiyu measured wealth and status, for the man that had many horses was respected and thought to be a great warrior. But now those same men were dead, their bodies disposed of by the Paiute who had defeated them and shamed their spirits by dumping them into a ravine and covered with dirt and rocks with no honor nor respect given.

Tauitau scowled as he waited to see the men that had fought with the Paiute, the two men that had the thunder weapons. The two men who were not native, but a white man and a man of dark skin that he and the others had thought to be an evil spirit that had great power. Tauitau cared little about the spirit being or whatever he might be, only that he had a weapon of great power, a weapon that would soon be his and restore his power among his people. His brother, Achekaia had scorned him as he left with the only warriors that survived to return to their people, but his brother had often stood against him, preferring to be hesitant in any action, while Tauitau believed it best to charge into the fray and kill those who resisted and take what was to be had, for those who were not of the Liksiyu were unworthy of thought or consideration and whatever they had was there to be taken by the stronger warriors, the Liksiyu! But the brothers had often conflicted with one another, more so than most brothers, and their fights, even as youngsters were vicious and resulted in injuries and scars. But Tauitau was determined to prove his brother wrong and show his people who was the greater warrior and leader, for when he returned with the great power of the thunder weapons, no one could stand before him!

He watched as the village resumed its usual daily activities, the women were preparing the harvest of piñon nuts, some were scraping hides, others were working on weaving baskets and some were busy at cookfires. The men had been busy with the bodies of the attackers, but now resumed working at fashioning weapons, flint knapping to craft points for arrows and lances, peeling willow or alder for arrows and bows, while others sat around talking about the fight. But from his vantage point, he could not discern the camp of the men with the thunder weapons, but he knew they could not leave the village without being seen. He would wait and watch, no matter how long it would require.

Tauitau's patience was soon rewarded when he saw riders come from the trees and brush on the far side of the river, and ride into the water to cross the rambling stream. He knew the crossing was where his warriors had crossed in the early morning as they carried out his plan of attack, the wide crossing had a solid bottom and was divided by a long sandbar, making the crossing easier than most. He watched as the two men, both in full buckskins which marked them as those that had the thunder weapons, and both leading pack horses, came from the river. He frowned, noticing the second pack horse was unusual, long ears like he had never seen before. He shook his head as he scooted back from the crest of the butte, *These are strange men, with different ways and weapons and even their animals are strange.*

He descended the butte, zigzagging across the face

of the steep slope, and out of habit, moved from tree to tree or brush for concealment, although there was no one to see him. As he came to the cluster of piñon and cedar where his horse was tethered, he stopped and dropped behind the trees, seeing someone with his horse. He watched long enough to recognize Tall Lance and was surprised that one of his warriors had returned and was waiting. Tauitau stood and walked through the trees, scowled at the man who stood, as he spoke, "I chose to follow you! Achekaia spoke against you, but I believe you are the greater warrior and leader. You seek to restore your power by taking those with the thunder weapons. I will go with you!" he declared, slapping his fist against his chest to avow his loyalty.

Tauitau was pleased but would not show it, believing he had to always show his strength and superiority before any that would follow. He scowled at the man, nodded, "You chose well! Come. The two with the thunder weapons are leaving the village of the Paiute, we will follow and when the time is right, we will take the power from them!"

Dusk was threatening when they were in the deep sage flats, the men they followed had broken from the sage into the grasslands and if they followed, they would be seen. Tauitau reined up at the edge of a tall sage. He had seen the two men split, one going into the marshland, the other continuing ahead. He paused a moment, searching the terrain for the two, and with a quick glance to Tall Lance, he motioned to the sage and they dropped from their mounts to seek cover behind the tall sage and wait for darkness.

A small patch of bunch grass offered graze for their horses, but there was no water. The men seated themselves on some rocks, dug into their pouches for some smoked meat and made do with what they had for the last meal of the day. Tauitau was anxious to attack the two strange men, but he was hesitant about how to make the assault. He glanced at Tall Lance, "We will attack together, after they are in their blankets. If we ride into their camp quickly, we can be upon them before they can rise and get to their weapons and we will drive our lances into them where they lay. They will not have their power in the night!"

"Have you not seen the black wolf? He travels with them and would know if we are near! And was it not these men that attacked our camp in the night with the snakes?" asked Tall Lance, his fear showing in his eyes.

"No! There was no white man! There were no thunder weapons then!" snarled Tauitau. Although he did believe they were the ones that attacked them, he would not admit it to Tall Lance. It was better that he did not know, for he was known to be a good warrior, but also a fearful one.

***

Gabe and Ezra enjoyed their leisurely meal, tossed a few scraps to Wolf and sat back to consider what to expect. "I'm pretty sure there's just one but could be a couple or more that might have followed further back. But no matter how many, I figger if we can fool 'em into thinkin' we don't know 'bout 'em, make it look like we're asleep in our blankets, we might lure 'em in and deal with 'em up close."

Ezra grinned, for his preferred fighting was 'up close' where he could see and strike his opponent. Maybe it was the enhanced danger and the suddenness of the fighting that stirred him, or just the ability to look them in the eye as he dealt his justice with the war club. Whatever it was, he had repeatedly proven himself to be a deadly adversary, not because he liked killing, he did not. But to render judgment on those that would do wrong was what he sought to deal with a powerful blow from his gavel of justice. Yet he was equally formidable with rifle, pistol and his other weapons, his preferred weapon was his war club.

The two men stood for a thorough survey of their camp and any approaches, wanting to anticipate and prepare for all possibilities. Gabe pointed, "If they come mounted, that's the only way. But if they come afoot, there, there and ... there," pointing as he turned and focused on each access.

"You talk as if there is a 'they' instead of just a 'he'," replied Ezra as he looked at the places indicated by Gabe. "Also, what about there," pointing to the small stream that fed the ponds. "There's a lotta water that direction, but it could be waded."

"Then let's picket the animals there, and they can warn us if anybody comes from that direction. We can pick our places accordingly."

Twilight offered just enough to see as they chose their places to await the attack, if there was to be one, and they arranged the camp to appear as if they were both in their blankets and sound asleep. They let the fire fade, leaving just the glow of coals, and Gabe had Wolf at his side as they crawled into the thicket of chokecherry brush. Ezra was opposite in the willows that overhung the stream on one side, and the grassy shoulder on the other. He was well hidden and if Gabe did not know where he was, there was nothing to give away his position. Gabe and Wolf were concealed in the brush that offered a good view of the camp, but deeper darkness within the shrubbery.

Now, they waited.

When silence fell and movement stopped, the bull-frogs renewed their chorus and the cicadas offered their accompaniment. The usual sounds of the night were normally comforting to Gabe, but the undertone of impending danger made the music of the nocturnal creatures somehow discordant. In the distance, coyotes lifted their yipping and howling, painting the darkness with their message of loneliness. A nighthawk added his oft-repeated squeal as he circled the marsh, looking for his supper. The full moon rose in the east, shedding its light on the plains, deepening the shadows of the trees around the camp.

Gabe shifted his weight, searching for a bit of comfort, when a low growl came from Wolf. The nearby creatures of the night had suddenly gone silent, and Gabe glanced down at the wolf, saw where he had focused his attention and turned his eyes to search the night shadows.

They burst from the trees at a run, screaming their war cries and charging into the camp with their high-stepping horses fighting the hackamore reins. Two warriors charged directly toward the blankets; lances lifted high, ready to plunge their points into their intended victims. Wolf leaped from the brush and launched himself at the nearest warrior, locked his teeth on his arm and knocking him from his horse. Gabe stood, pistol in hand, searching for a target, but Wolf had taken him to the ground. Ezra's pistol barked and Gabe heard the ball crash through the branches and leaves overhead.

The lead warrior drove his lance into the blankets beneath the stomping hooves of his horse, and when the pistol barked, he flinched, fell forward on the horse's neck and dug his heels into the mount's ribs to drive him from the camp. He crashed through the trees, the riderless horse following and disappeared into the darkness. Wolf tore at the man on the ground, growling and snarling. The man screamed, but his cry was cut short when Wolf's teeth locked on his throat. With another snarl as he jerked his head side to side, Wolf ripped the throat from the man, leaving a trembling and bloody mess at his feet. The beast spat the mass of flesh from his mouth, snarled at the prone figure, until he heard Gabe call, then spun and trotted back to the side of his friend.

Gabe looked up as Ezra started toward him, both men searching the trees for another charge, but the woods were quiet. "You were right, there were two of 'em," declared Ezra. "I think I hit that'n that took off, but not too bad."

"No, if you hit him, it was just a graze, cuz I heard the bullet whip through the leaves overhead."

Ezra looked at the still figure near their blankets, "That'n ain't goin' nowhere. Wolf made sure of that." He reached down to stroke the wolf's scruff, then looked up at Gabe, "You think we'd be safe gettin' some sleep?"

"Prob'ly. You go ahead. I'll drag that'n outta here

and sit up a spell, just in case."

"If you get tired, wake me."

Gabe nodded as he replaced the pistol in his belt, then went to the carcass to drag it into the brush, well away from the camp to let the carrion eaters, that would find it soon enough, have their way.

22 / SIGN

With an early start, they were on the trail when the first grey line showed off their right shoulder. As the sky began to show color, they had traveled about four or five miles and were brought to a stop as they stared at the ground before them. When they traversed this land just a few days before, it was thick with tall grasses and scattered rabbit brush, sage, and greasewood, but now it looked like a legion of farmers had come through with their teams and plows. Gabe stood in his stirrups looking to the east, north and west, seeing the wide swath of churned soil leaving a broad scar that pointed to the west and southwest. He looked at Ezra, "That's buffalo!" and stepped to the ground. He walked into the tracks, the soil had been churned and trampled, and he looked at Ezra, "That was a big herd, not massive, mind you, but big!"

"But what're they doin' goin' that way? Lone Bear

said the herds had already started south and east, making their migration."

"I dunno, but every track there, and they're fresh enough, no more'n a day old, is headin' thataway," he turned to look along the long swath that pointed toward the higher mountains. He frowned, "Ya know, that appears to be the direction of the valley we came down. Maybe they're headin' up there. There's lotsa grass, water, and it sure would make a good hunt!" He chuckled as he stepped back aboard Ebony, grinning at Ezra.

"Yeah, but that puzzles me as to why they're doin' just the opposite of what they normally do. Ya don't suppose somethin's drivin' 'em do ya?"

"What would be big enough or scary enough to stampede a big herd of buffalo?"

Ezra shook his head, "Dunno, fire maybe." The thought of a prairie fire prompted both men to stand in their stirrups and look back along the swath of trampled soil but saw nothing.

"Reckon we better get the word to Spotted Eagle. They'll be glad to hear the buffalo haven't all gone."

It was midafternoon as they crossed the grasslands, the distant line of mountains beckoning, when they noticed a low-lying dark cloud to the east. It was more of a shadow, and spread across the flats, covering the wide swath of grass prairie that showed to the east.

"Now what do you s'pose that is," asked Ezra, scowling at the phenomenon. It appeared to be at least three or four miles distant yet moving.

"Dunno, but I don't like the looks of it. What say we get a move on and get to Spotted Eagles's camp. Might hafta take cover or somethin'," suggested Gabe.

They slapped legs to the horses and took off at a canter. They had lead lines on the pack animals, and they were stretched out until they matched the pace of the ridden horses. It was just a couple miles to the village, but they saw many of the villagers, afoot and busy at edge of the creek. Several of the men were busy digging what appeared to be semi-circular ditches, women were wading in the creek, baskets in hand, and a frowning Gabe and Ezra reined up beside Spotted Eagle who sat horseback, watching the workers. Everyone was busy but looked up often in the direction of the low-lying cloud.

Gabe asked, "What is goin' on?" looking from the women in the creek and the men busy at the trenches. Several boys and girls came with armloads of cut grasses, the long stems of the rushes and sedges, most of it dry and brown. The men stepped down, stood beside their horses and Spotted Eagle explained, "That," pointing to the distant shadow, "is bread bugs, what you call crickets. The trenches will be covered with the grasses, the crickets will fall in and we will fire the grass to roast the bugs." He pointed to the women,

"The bugs will cover the water, the current will carry them into the baskets, and they will be gathered."

"But what for?" asked a bewildered Ezra.

"They will be roasted, ground into a flour, and added to the breads. It makes a very good bread." He smiled at the expression on Ezra's face.

Gabe looked back to the east, "They're gettin' close, I can hear 'em now. Shouldn't we get somewhere?"

"Yes!" declared Spotted Eagle as he swung aboard his mount, he shouted to the people, "To the camp!" and they dropped what they were doing and started running toward the camp. The tipis and brush huts were clustered back from the mouth of the valley and would hopefully be out of the path of the horde. The sound was a low hissing buzz that became louder and sounded like a clattering hum. The cloud of crickets now showed as a low lying but moving cloud, thinner at the top edge, almost black near the ground.

Gabe and Ezra fought the skittish horses and the pack animals, dragging them on taut leads as they drove to the valley. The men did not slow until they were past most of the lodges, then took to the trees on the west edge, and under cover of the pines, stopped and began stripping the gear from the animals. They tethered the animals on a long lead, giving them access to both water and graze, and once they were certain the animals were safe, the men returned to the lower end of the camp where the villagers were congregated to watch the invading horde of armored bugs.

The sound of the clattering was almost deafening, and they had to shout to be heard above the roar. The cloud of locust type creatures crept slowly west and southwest across the grassy flats. The stream that came from the valley of the camp, twisted its way through the willows and alders into the grassy plains and was now covered in the dark blanket of insects. As they watched, it moved like a rolling wave, each layer overtaken by another and another, consuming everything in its path.

Ravens, magpies, hawks, and owls swooped into the horde, coming from the cloud with mouthfuls of helmeted creatures that also grabbed onto the feathers and hitched a free ride as the birds lifted-up and away. Coyotes were running into the cloud, mouths open, gobbling everything that passed their teeth.

The creatures overran the trenches, weighting down the grasses and filling the trench, only to be used as bridges for the next wave that kept moving. The stream became a tide of black and brown, sweeping waves of bugs into the baskets and overloading them. And still they came. The racketing of their noisemakers drowning any effort to talk to one another and the tide surged into the valley. Men and women broke off branches of juniper and slapped at the hopping and crawling menace, some of them as big as a man's finger, three inches long and just as fat, beating them back even as they hopped onto the clothing and the branches.

Gabe and Ezra had also grabbed some branches to aid in the effort of turning back the onslaught and as it seemed to ebb, they stood, staring at the unbeliev-able sight as the grassland had disappeared under the mass. But as they looked to the east, it appeared the tide was lessening, the cloud was thinning, and the noise slowly subsiding. Gabe looked at Ezra, "This is what drove the buffalo back!"

"Buffalo?" asked Spotted Eagle, "You found buffalo?"

Gabe chuckled, "Yeah. The Paiute told us the herds had already started south and east on the migration route, but we crossed a wide trail of 'em this mornin'," he pointed with his chin back to the south, "and they were headin' west in a hurry. Now we understand why," nodding to the mass of crickets. "I never thought I'd see the day when an entire herd of buffalo would run from a bunch of crickets, but . . ." he shook his head in wonder.

The horde continued, but seemed less, and left nothing in its wake. The grass had been stripped to the ground, the sage stood as twisted skeletons, other brush was devoid of any green and the only thing seemingly untouched was the cholla and prickly pear cactus, although some of the prickly pear had chunks missing from the broad blades and some of the spines held skewered crickets. When the din abated, all the villagers returned to the trenches and the creek to retrieve the baskets full of drowned crickets. The trenches were fired, and the burrows of bugs were roasted under the flames. Those taken from the water would be spread out on the trail and other hardened ground to let the sun dry and roast the harvest.

The word spread about the herd of buffalo and everyone hustled about to tend to the crickets but were chattering about the coming hunt. After the report of Gabe and Ezra, Spotted Eagle dispatched scouts on fresh horses to seek out the buffalo and return to lead the rest of the hunters to the wooly beasts. There was a light mood in the camp of the people, everyone chattering and laughing, women working together, some at the cook fires, others busy with the crickets, laying them out for the drying process and some to be roasted, others returning to the trenches for more baskets full.

Gabe asked Spotted Eagle, "So, they dry 'em and roast 'em then grind 'em to a powder?"

Eagle chuckled at his friend, "It is a delicacy and very nutritious. When there were no buffalo, our people spent these last days gathering many baskets of camas, and we were pleased for this land was rich with the camas. Then we thought the Creator had sent the bread bugs to also see us through the winter. I have never seen this before, but my people tell of it happening long ago. Where we usually live, the crickets have not come, it is this land of grass and sage that is hot and dry that brings the crickets."

"Well, I don't think you can convince me those bugs are as good as a fresh buffalo steak!"

Eagle laughed, "But you see, my friend, the Creator has used the crickets to bring the buffalo back to us, so we will enjoy both!"

Unseen by Gabe and Ezra, across the flats beyond the swath left by the crickets, a lone man hunkered in a deep ravine, anger blazing in his eyes and determination welling up within his spirit. Tauitau spat at his feet, slid down the bank of the ravine to the trickling stream where his horse drank deeply, and mumbled to himself, "*I will have his power! Nothing will stop me!*"

23 / BUFFALO

It was two days until the scouts returned and the dancing began. The people that just a few days before were despondent and fearful now had much to celebrate. The Creator had gifted them with a bounty of bugs and buffalo and tomorrow would see the camp moved nearer the herd and the hunt would begin. Gabe and Ezra sat near Spotted Eagle and watched the dancers mimic the buffalo and the hunters. Several of the women had donned pieces of buffalo hide and used their fingers to imitate the horns of the buffalo and they danced with heads down and shuffling step while the men pursued showing great feats of courage as they chased down the women/buffalo and downed them with a thrust of their lance. The drums beat a steady cadence and the chanting and shouting added to the joviality. This was not a time of feasting, that would come after a successful hunt, but it was a time of celebration.

"We will leave before first light. The scouts say it will be a long day of travel," declared Spotted Eagle, glancing to his friends.

"That's the way we came. It's a grassy valley, good water, broad flat. But that's also where the *Waiilatpus* hit the camp of the Paiute."

Eagle frowned at Ezra, "Is that where you danced with the snakes?"

Ezra chuckled, "You might say that, I didn't exactly dance with 'em, sorta threw 'em on the sleepers and let them do the dancin'."

The men laughed at the remembrance and Gabe frowned, "You know, I been wonderin' if that fella followin' us was one o' them that hit the camp of the Paiute and danced with the snakes."

"Could be, that'd explain why he's so all fired mad at us."

"Who is following you?" asked Spotted Eagle.

"That's just it, we don't rightly know. But when we were comin' back to join you, a couple that looked to be Waiilatpus, jumped us in the night. Wolf took down one of 'em, but the other'n got away with a flesh wound. But they sure tried to do us in, poked our blankets full of holes with their lances!"

"Are you still followed?" asked Eagle.

"Dunno. Haven't seen any sign of him, but I reckon we'll find out soon enough."

Most often it is the patient hunter that gains the trophy. And when the hunted is man, the need for patience is magnified, for when the hunter becomes the hunted, he is often more wary than the cagiest of wild animals. The greater the beast, the less often he is hunted, and the more he tends to assume he will not be, but a man experienced in the wild who knows he is hunted, seeks to become the hunter. Both Gabe and Ezra had been both hunter and hunted and both knew the pitfalls of assuming anything about the hunter.

Tauitau had watched the camp of the Salish from afar, remembering this was the band his people attacked under the direction of the shaman, Pale Eagle. He remembered the terrible toll they paid in lost and wounded warriors when they were turned back by the power of the thunder weapons. But he grinned as he watched, knowing there were those within this band that had the weapons he sought and if he could not take those from the white man and his friend, perhaps he could take one or more from the Salish. Tauitau had built his reputation as a fierce warrior on his ability to sneak into an enemy's camp and take coups, and even take scalps, without anyone knowing until the next light. He had even shown his own people his ability at stealth by sneaking into their lodges and taking some trophy while they were sleeping.

He was well hidden in the trees near the top of

the butte west of and overlooking the camp of the Salish and watched as they danced and celebrated. He could tell by the dance that mimicked the buffalo, they were anticipating a buffalo hunt, and what better time would there be than to strike during the hunt, where no one would be looking for an outsider to infiltrate their camp or their hunters. He watched until most were settled in for the night, then turned in to his blankets to wait for his opportunity.

The band was well on their way come first light. With the rising sun at their back, the flat land sage gave little in the way of protection with most of the greenery stripped by the crickets. By mid-day they were into the grass lands that lay south of the path of the crickets and the greenery was a welcome change as horses snatched mouthfuls as they walked and the dew that remained from the early morning was cooling to the moccasined feet of the travelers. Although the men rode, many of the women walked and led the horses that trailed the travois laden with the makings of shelters and the trappings of the people. These same travois would hopefully soon be loaded with mounds of fresh buffalo meat and more, promising ample food for the cold season.

They passed the hot springs with their plumes of steam that lifted to the blue sky of the warm day and by late afternoon they rounded the point of the long

ridge that came from the lower mountains on the
north of the valley. Eagle pushed on to lead the people to make their camp beside the creek as it wound
its way near the edge of the alluvial fans spreading
into the valley from the high mountains. The valley
showed green mottled with browns and reds, tall
grasses waving in the early evening breeze and in the
distance, further up the valley, the brown blanket of
the buffalo herd lay across the flats.

The long valley was framed on the north and south
by the finger ridges and mountains of what would one
day be called the Beaverhead and Lemhi mountains.
The sun was lowering over the southwest mountains,
dropping the curtain of dusk, and coloring the valley
with the golden tint of day's end. Eagle directed the
people as they began settling in to what would be
their temporary camp, but where they would do the
early work of butchering, smoking, and scraping any
buffalo taken. The meat and by-products would need
to be prepared before they began the long journey to
return to their winter encampment.

"We go to scout the herd, will you come?" asked
Spotted Eagle, speaking to Gabe and Ezra.

"Of course!" responded Gabe. A quick glance to
Ezra and the two friends went to their horses, preparing to join the leader of the Salish and the others.

The small band numbered eight including Gabe
and Ezra, and they rode into the valley, hugging

the north edge as the creek crowded them closer to the steep slopes of the foothills. The buffalo milled around on the upper reaches of the lower part of the valley. A natural barrier of a low ridge and difficult terrain divided the long valley into the upper and lower valleys, and the herd had pushed close to the low ridge but seemed content to graze the deep grass beside the meandering stream.

The scouts stopped where the creek pushed against the talus slope of the steep sided mountain that rose fifteen hundred feet above the valley floor. The north edge of the valley was lined with similar mountains for a stretch of about five miles. Spotted Eagle led the way as they climbed to a shoulder above the talus and dropped to their haunches to scout the herd. Gabe slipped his scope from the case and stretched it out to take a better look and drew curious stares from the others. Ezra glanced at his friend, chuckled, and turned back to survey the terrain and the movement of the herd.

The three to four mile wide valley was deep with grasses, rabbit brush and grease wood, with the wide alluvial fans, the formation made when years of water flow from higher mountains carries sand, silt and soil to fan out on the valley floor, held sparse patches of grasses, wheat grass, wildrye, needlegrass and cheatgrass. Sage dotted the fans, while the deeper and greener grasses populated the stretches nearer the creek bed.

Eagle pointed, "We will have mounted hunters sweep across the far edge, then come at the herd from there," pointing to the west end of the dividing ridge. "Those with rifles will be along the stream, in the brush and hidden, and as the herd passes, they will shoot." He pointed to a shoulder at the edge of the alluvial formation that bordered the deeper grass of the creek flat, "Others could be there, along that rise."

The other scouts looked as Eagle pointed, nodding agreement, and mentally picking the spot or place where they would be or if they were mounted, how they would ride the herd. Gabe said, "It looks like, once the herd is on the move, they'll run near the creek, prob'ly cross it down there," pointing to a spot where the creek bent away from the mountains and into the valley, "and maybe keep goin' through that stretch."

The others looked from Gabe to Eagle and to the valley below, visualizing the movement of the herd. They looked at one another, back to Eagle and mumbled their agreement. Eagle grinned, "I think it will be a good hunt. I will be with the riders, where will you two be?"

Gabe looked to Ezra and Ezra responded, "I think I'll be down there along the creek. It's a bit difficult to reload that long barreled Lancaster while I'm riding a horse that's fighting for space with a big bull."

Gabe chuckled and looked at Spotted Eagle, "Ezra's right about that, but I will be wherever I can do the most good. We," nodding to Ezra, "won't have any trouble getting the two we need, but if you would like more for your people, then you tell me where I can help."

"But if you do not want to reload your rifle on horseback, what else would you do?" asked Eagle, glancing from Gabe to his scope and back.

"I can shoot my bow well enough from horseback, and as you know, nocking another arrow is not that difficult."

"We will decide in the morning." He paused, looked at the scope again, "What does that do?" asked Eagle, frowning.

Gabe grinned as he stretched out the scope and demonstrated, "Hold it to your eye, like this, and move it to see what you want." He handed it to Eagle and watched as he slowly looked through the long scope, then jerked back and looked around, glanced at Gabe and frowning, put it back to his eye. He moved it slowly side to side and grinned as he grew accustomed to what he was seeing. He lowered it and looked at Gabe, "That is strange."

"Not really, it's just these pieces of glass that are shaped the way they are and work together," he explained as he pushed the scope together and placed it in its case. Eagle looked at the man, a slight frown wrinkling his forehead, and with a shake of his head, he stood and led the others down the slope to the horses.

24 / HUNT

The air was full of excitement and anticipation, the people were up and about before first light. Fires were lit to give the hunters a hot meal and to give light for everyone that was busy with the preparations. The men had gathered the horses and were busy with their individual mounts. Several were painting the horses with the markings that would bring good hunting. Men had dipped their hands in the paints made with vermillion, chalk, dried flowers and more, and put their hand prints on the shoulders of their favored horse used for a buffalo hunt. Their choice being their fleetest animal, strong and confident, and trained to be maneuvered with leg pressure. The hunters that were selected to take to the brush and lie in ambush were busy cleaning their rifles, loading, and priming the weapons, or stringing their bows and examining each of the arrows for the fletching, point and strength. Some men and several women sat sharpening their knives and tomahawks in anticipation of the butchering. Most had done their preparations the night before but were busy with last-minute details.

Gabe and Ezra rode into the camp, looking around at the busyness, and looked up to see Spotted Eagle walking toward them. "You are ready!" he declared, smiling.

"We are ready," responded Gabe, as he stepped down to stand before the leader of the Salish. Ezra joined them as they looked about the camp and the many people excitedly readying themselves and their animals.

Spotted Eagle looked at Gabe, "Will you ride with us?"

"If that's where you want me, yes."

"We will lead the approach to the herd, we will begin the chase!" he grinned at the thought. The excitement and danger of any buffalo hunt stirred the blood of a man that knew what lay before him. The chase, the shooting of the arrow, the thrust of the lance, all while at an all-out run beside a beast that had the strength, weight, and speed to trample you and your mount under and could destroy you with a simple lunge or charge, made a man more alive at that moment than any other. Each of these men had experienced that rush, that fear, that excitement and knew what awaited them on this day.

Several of the hunters had drawn near, and Spotted Eagle motioned for the others to join. As the group grew, they crowded closer and Spotted Eagle lifted his hands for quiet. He began, "Spirit Bear will ride with me and we will lead the hunt. Running Wolf and Black Buffalo will lead the shooters from the creek." He looked to Running Wolf, "Keep your horses near so you can join the hunt as it passes, if you choose." Running Wolf glanced from Eagle to Ezra and nodded his agreement. Eagle continued, "We ask that Coyote and the Creator give us a good hunt!" He lifted his hands and motioned for the hunters to mount.

They rode by the light of the lowering moon and the few stars that remained in the late-night sky. They took to the alluvial plains with the grasses and sage, keeping away from the bottom of the valley where any wandering animals might be going to the creek for their morning drink. Wolf was trotting between his friends and Gabe looked down at his furry friend. The wolf sensed the attention and turned to look up at Gabe. "You're goin' with Ezra, so keep him safe, understand?" he asked, as if the animal would answer. But the two had an understanding of one another and Gabe was confident Wolf did understand.

It was just beginning to show light off their right shoulder, when the two groups parted, Ezra and Wolf went with the creek shooters moving through the deep grass and across the valley to the brush lined creek, while the others kept to the higher plains. As the grey of morning began silhouetting the mountains, they neared the herd. They stopped and Spotted Eagle motioned toward a dry gulch that marked the base of the long ridge that divided the valley. They were above and somewhat behind the herd, and the band of hunters nudged their mounts to drop over the edge and into the gulch. As they rode in the sandy bottom, Eagle stationed men along the edge, readying them to assault the herd as a united front, giving each man an equal chance to make the coveted first kill.

Tauitau watched from his camp in the trees as the band of hunters split, but he focused his attention on those that rode below him. He had made his camp in the dark of night, choosing a point where the trees offered good cover, and the high point gave a good view of the valley. Always a light sleeper, the silence that hushes the night sounds brought him awake, and he rose to see the hunters pass. He grinned, waiting for their passing, then led his horse as he took to a slight depression that led to the creek below. Probably formed in some spring that saw an excessive amount of snowfall and the runoff pushed its way through the sandy soil, it gave Tauitau good cover for this moonlit early morning.

It was easy for him to see the tactic that would be used in the hunt, the lay of the land dictated the

movements of the herd and the hunters, and Tauitau
chose the point where he would join the thundering
herd and the many hunters that would be looking at
nothing but the buffalo. He grinned as he envisioned
his moves that would take him near the man with the
thunder weapons. He would be easy to see with his
black horse and full buckskins, and just as easy to kill.

Gabe and Spotted Eagle were the last two and Eagle
turned his mount to face the bank of the gulch. Down
the line behind them, the hunters waited and watched,
weapons at the ready, and Eagle slowly mounted the
bank, Gabe doing the same. As he neared the crest,
seeing the herd close in, he raised his free arm overhead and signaled. The men dug heels to their horses'
ribs and lunged up the bank. The sudden movement
startled the buffalo and the herd seemed to move as
one, lifting the massive heads and swinging them
away as they started to run. The hunters were instantly among them, screaming and shouting, and chasing
their chosen target.

   Gabe quickly made his choice of a lone cow and
nudged Ebony to the chase. The big black responded,
stretching out his head, mane and tail flying in the
wind, Gabe leaning into the charge, his Mongol bow
clasped firmly with a finger of the nocked arrow. The
long-legged stallion seemed to stretch out more, his
thundering hooves beating a cadence that rivaled

that of the herd, and with each lunge, drew closer to the wooly beast. The maddening cacophony of the stampede rolled like thunderclaps. Dirt, grass, dust flying as cloven hooves dug deep to drive the thousand-pound monsters down the valley. Ebony's shoulder was beside the hip of the cow, each step bringing him closer, within but a breath, they were near and Gabe brought the bow to full draw, gripping the stallion with his legs, toes driving into the stirrups, and with a deep breath, he drew it just an inch more, and let the arrow fly. It seemed to flutter through the air that lay between them, but the instant was fleeting, and the black shaft was buried to the fletching into the low chest of the cow. Gabe quickly nudged Ebony away and the buffalo stumbled, dropped its head to the ground and flipped end over end.

Gabe nocked another arrow, looking for his next target. His quick glance told him they were already nearing the point where the shooters were waiting, and he moved Ebony away from that side of the herd. He saw others had taken their first shot and several carcasses littered the churned soil behind them. He quickly chose another target, a young bull and gave chase. Ebony sensed the chosen bull and stretched out again. The racketing of rifle fire nudged the herd closer to the shoulder ridge that paralleled the creek, crowding the herd closer, but several had fallen to the fire of the shooters and Gabe kept his eyes on the young bull.

The herd charged ahead, flattening everything in its path. The shoulder from the alluvial plains began to rise and the herd continued to side the creek. They lumbered over the edge of the shoulder, appearing like a wave of brown as they moved in unison. Gabe and Ebony gave chase, as did the other mounted hunters.

A quick glance showed several riders barely visible through the heavy dust, but they moved with the herd. The young bull pushed into a close bunch of cows, that crowded their yearling calves ahead, and as Ebony neared, the bull veered to the right just enough to force Ebony to the left of the bull. It would be an awkward shot, requiring Gabe to twist around in his saddle and take the shot earlier from further behind, but he was determined to down the bull. Suddenly the bull stumbled and Ebony shot forward alongside the beast and Gabe twisted in his saddle, saw another hunter on the far side of the bull, and as he started his draw, the Indian reined his mount against the bull, driving him into Ebony. The bull jerked his head up, bellowed, his tongue lolling from the open mouth, and then dropped his head. As Gabe again started his draw, the bull swung into Ebony, lifted his head, and snagged the stirrup leather of Gabe's saddle and jerked up, his horn catching Gabe's buckskins and throwing him off his horse.

Gabe felt himself flying through the cloud of dust, had an instant thought that this was gonna hurt, and tumbled into the dust and dirt, after bouncing off the back of the wooly cow. With hooves of buffalo thundering past, he was struck by another, tumbled end over end, felt the strike of several hooves on his leg and back and blackness shrouded his sight and everything was still and silent. While he lay still, the herd and hunters rumbled past, shrouding him in the dirt and dust of the aftermath of their passing, but he was unaware of anything, only the deep black that enveloped him.

25 / RECOVERY

Ezra had picked a young bull, watching as the herd roared past, buffalo tossing their heads, most with heads down bellowing, tongues lolling, and blindly following the mass before them, unable to see anything but the brown of the beasts, the grey of the dust, and the dirt clods and grass clumps flying. The bull hung to the side, and Ezra lined up his sights as he neared, followed the running beast and squeezed off the shot. The long rifle bucked, spat smoke and lead, and Ezra peered through the smoke to see the shadowy image stumble and bury its nose in the dirt, sliding to a stop. He instantly brought the rifle down and started reloading, watching the herd rumble past. He stretched up with the ramrod, drove the ball and patch to be seated, and with horn in hand, primed the pan and snapped it shut. He eared back the hammer as he lifted his weapon to his shoulder, looking for another target, but the dust gave way just enough to see a buckskin clad figure take flight over the passing humps.

He recognized Gabe and had a passing thought as to why he was trying to fly, then he was shrouded in dust and wooly beasts. Ezra jumped to his feet, turned, and grabbed the reins of his bay gelding and swung aboard. He saw Wolf disappear into the dust as he searched for a break in the herd so he could go to his friend. His heart beat so hard he thought it was fighting free of his chest, he snatched a breath, stood in his stirrups to look into the melee.

A mounted Indian had turned back and appeared to be looking for Gabe also, as the stragglers of the herd lumbered by and Ezra gigged his bay across the creek. The horse splashed water high as Ezra leaned along the animal's neck, and quickly climbed the low bank from the water. Ezra saw Ebony return to the side of Gabe, then he frowned as he saw the Indian approaching the prone figure of Gabe with his knife unsheathed as he glared at the buckskinned man.

Ezra's thoughts gave alarm as he recognized the Indian as the same man that charged through their camp and tried to kill them. He dropped the reins on the bay's neck, brought his rifle to his shoulder and dropped the hammer. The rifle roared and belched smoke, as Ezra slapped legs to the bay to charge to the aid of his friend. He saw the Indian flinch, look

up and glance around, and step to Ebony and snatch
the rifle from its scabbard. He looked at the man
on the ground, jumped back when a big black wolf
suddenly straddled the man and snarled at Tauitau.
He lunged for his own horse, swung aboard and
slapped legs to chase after the herd, disappearing
into the lingering dust cloud.

Ezra slid the bay to a stop and hit the ground running. He dropped to the ground beside Gabe, quickly
looking him over, saw the prints of cloven hooves, dirt
and smudges, blood at his leg, then turned him over.
His head was bruised and bleeding where a hoof had
slammed into his scalp, ripping it back and showing
bone. His face was bleeding from several contusions,
bruises were already showing, lumps were growing,
but for what he had been through, Ezra thought *He
doesn't look as bad as I expected.* He saw Gabe's chest
intermittently rise and fall, was relieved, but concerned. He glanced up at Ebony and saw the empty
scabbard, glimpsed around and saw the Mongol bow
had been under Gabe and appeared undamaged. The
saddle pistols still hung in the holsters at the saddle's
pommel, and the belt pistol and tomahawk had stayed
secure in Gabe's belt, probably causing more bruises
as he landed on them.

Gabe's breathing was ragged as Ezra poured water
over his face and wiped some of the blood off. He was
surprised when he heard Wolf growl, then looked at

him and back to where he was looking. A big bull was standing about thirty yards off, head lowered, chest heaving, and glaring at the wolf. The bull dug his front hoof into the dirt, dragged it back and tossed the dirt into the air. He repeated the action with his other hoof, and Ezra knew the beast was about to charge. He snatched up his rifle, brought it to bear as he eared back the hammer, and squeezed off the shot just as the bull lunged forward. He had aimed just to the side of the bull's chin, hoping to score a hit on the chest and maybe hit the heart, but the lunge made the bullet cut a groove across the shoulder and plow along the rib cage of the bull.

The charging bull kept coming, lumbering, and humping with every lunge, Ezra frantically started to reload the rifle, but grabbed his belt pistol instead. He lifted it with his right hand, felt at Gabe's belt for his pistol, and fired his, then Gabe's in quick succession. He aimed for the eyes of the beast, knowing the chances of dropping the bull with the pistols was improbable. He saw the impact of the bullets as he swiveled both barrels and cocked the second hammers, he lifted them again and fired then rolled over the body of Gabe to protect his friend. He heard Wolf Growl and snarl, heard the impact of the bull as it hit the ground, then looked to see the wolf, teeth locked on the nose of the bull and shaking it as if were nothing but a scrawny jackrabbit. The bull had fallen on his side and was struggling to get up, and Wolf released his grip on the nose, jumped over the downed bull, and buried his teeth into the exposed gut of the bull.

Ezra jumped up to grab the saddle pistols, snatched them free and turned, bringing both hammers on both pistols to full cock. He stepped closer, pulled both triggers on both pistols and the weapons barked with a roar like thunder, blossomed smoke, and spat four .62 caliber balls at almost point-blank range. The impact sounded like the beating of war drum, and blood instantly sprang from the chest of the beast as it gave one slow grunt and fell back, stilled in death.

Wolf continued his assault, ripping open the beast's gut, and tearing it wide. He seized a mouthful of flesh, and stepped back, meat, blood, and slobber dripping as he glared at the head of the beast, then dropped to his belly to enjoy his bounty.

Ezra looked at Gabe, saw him breathing more regularly, and chose to reload the weapons. There could be more stragglers of the herd, each one on the prod, maybe wounded, and looking for something to take out their anger and vengeance on, man or beast. It was always best to be prepared. He replaced the pistols, leaned his rifle on the carcass of the buffalo and turned back to Gabe. He used the wet cloth to clean him up a little, lifting his shirt to examine his wounds, sliding up the legs of his britches to check his legs, and then sat back to wait and decide what to do next.

Spotted Eagle and Running Wolf rode up, slid down and looked from Gabe to Ezra, eyebrows lifted to ask the question. Ezra answered, "I dunno. His horse was hit by a bull, he got tossed, I saw him doing a poor imitation of a hawk, and then he got trampled some, but I think he'll be alright, if he wakes up."

Gabe was stirred by the conversation and struggled to open his eyes. He moaned as consciousness returned with the pain and his first word was, "Oooo-hh, what happened?"

"You tried to imitate a buzzard and took flight. You did alright till it came to the landing," explained Ezra, somber faced.

Gabe said, "Don't! It hurts too much," grabbing at his side. He reached to his head, his hand came back bloody, then glanced at Ezra, "Somebody try to scalp me?"

"Ummhmm, that same one that tried to skewer us in camp! He was getting ready to lift your hair but my Lancaster," he patted the rifle beside him, "convinced him otherwise. But I think I just grazed him, again, and he grabbed your Ferguson and took off!"

Gabe looked over at Ebony, who stood watching the men around his man, saw the empty scabbard, and said, "Where'd he go?"

"He took off thataway, prob'ly goin' back where he came from, but you ain't goin' nowhere till we get one o' those women to sew your topknot back on! And maybe look you over for anything else that needs tendin' too. Don't forget, you just got hooked an' run over by a whole herd of buffalo and you might need to heal up a mite."

Gabe rolled to the side and started working at rising, moaning, groaning, and struggling, until Ezra stood and offered to help. He strove to rise, and once erect, arched his back, and moaned some more, squinting in pain. He stood straight, lifted his hand to his side and moaned, "Prob'ly got some cracked ribs and my ankle's twisted. But other'n that, I think I'll live to try to fly again!"

Spotted Eagle stepped close, reaching up to examine the wound at his head, then said, "My woman will fix that, but it will hurt." He grinned, "I think she likes to make pain."

"Oh, now that's encouraging," replied Gabe, looking around. At the lower end of the killing fields, the women were already coming with horses and travois to being the butchering. "She coming?" he asked, nodding toward the women.

Eagle nodded, "I will go get her," he paused, pointed to the creek with his chin, "You go there, wash, wait."

Gabe nodded, watched Eagle and Running Wolf leave, then turned to Ezra, "I didn't do that, did I?" nodding to the downed buffalo where Wolf lay, contentedly licking his lips and his paws.

"No, it was kind of a joint effort. He was one of

the stragglers, and . . ." Ezra described the charge of the bull and what was done to bring him down, as they walked, leading their horses, to the creek. Gabe leaned against Ebony, hand holding the saddle horn for help, as he limped on his twisted ankle to the stream. They sat on the bank and Gabe slid his feet and ankles into the water, knowing the cold water would give some relief. He accepted the rag from Ezra and began working at his other wounds, washing away both dirt and blood. The cold cloth felt good on his face as he turned to look at Ezra. "So, as soon as I get sewed up, I'm goin' after that skunk that took my rifle. You comin'?"

Ezra chuckled, "I don't believe you'd think you had to ask!" The two life-long friends had seldom been separated, and never when one or the other was in need. This qualified as a need.

"But what about the buffalo we killed? We're gonna need that meat this winter!"

"I think we can prob'ly get Spotted Eagle to drop it off at the cabin for us, ya think?"

"I reckon. How many did you shoot?"

"Just one, 'fore that one there," pointing to the bull taken down by him and Wolf. "You?"

"One, until that one tried to hook me, but he was on the right side an' I couldn't turn around to get him with the bow." He looked at Ebony who stood beside Ezra's bay, munching on the grass. "At least I still have

my bow," he grumbled, thinking about his rifle. It had
been a favorite weapon of his father's extensive collection and was a rare breech-loading rifle. "I wonder
about that skunk that took it, I know he won't know
how to load it or anything, even if he has the makings.
I put my powder horn and possibles bag in the saddle
bags so I would be free to use my bow, so he didn't get
that, and as I remember what Lone Bear said, those
Waiilatpus don't have any rifles and probably won't
know what to do with it."

"Spotted Eagle said none of the attackers had rifles
and he thought they were surprised when the Salish
cut down on 'em with rifles. Could be that's what he's
been after, thinking he could figger it out on his own,"
suggested Ezra.

They both turned when they heard the approach
of horses, saw Running Wolf and Spotted Eagle with
his woman on behind him. She slid to the ground,
a parfleche in her hands and looked at Gabe with a
frown and came near. She drew close, looked at the
wound at his scalp, then directed him, "Lay down,
head that way so we can wash clean. Then I sew."

Gabe nodded, twisted around, and lay on his back,
his head toward the water. She splashed water on his
scalp, rinsing the wound, then dabbed it dry with a
clean cloth. She reached back to her parfleche and
brought out a handful of dried plants, handed them
to Ezra and said, "Make poultice."

Ezra nodded, wide-eyed, dipped the plants in water and began to mash them into a pulp on a nearby stone, and squeezed out the excess moisture and lay the handful on a piece of buckskin laid aside by the woman for that purpose. She knelt next to Gabe's head, brought out a thin piece of tendon, as fine as a piece of hair, a needle and reached for the wound. Within moments, after some squirming and wincing by Gabe, she finished, looked at her work, then nodded and stood. She looked at Spotted Eagle, "Take me to the others." Without a glance back, they rode off to join the other women at the butchering.

Gabe chuckled, "Doesn't talk much, does she?"

"Nope," declared Ezra. "While she was workin' on you, I told Spotted Eagle what we were plannin' and he said they'd take care of the meat for us and if we weren't back 'fore they left, they'd take it to the cabin."

"Then let's get back to our camp, get the rest of our gear, and see if we can catch up to that renegade that stole my rifle!"

26 / CHASE

Every step of the big stallion was felt by Gabe, even though Ebony's gait was long and smooth and normally appreciated by his rider, Gabe's many wounds and injuries transmitted every step, every roll, every hesitation, and each one seemed magnified in his pain. He purposefully shut out the consciousness of his discomfort, focusing instead on the tracks they followed and purpose for their pursuit.

The Ferguson rifle gave Gabe an advantage over any adversary, with the breech-loader he could fire the weapon seven times a minute which was double the firepower of a typical muzzle loaded flintlock. But it wasn't just the weapon's advantage, it was the sentimental connection to his dead father, for it had been a treasured and favorite part of his extensive firearms collection and the preferred weapon of Gabe since his father first allowed him to fire the rifle. And the thought of this warrior of the Waiilatpus that had been a part of the carnage of the Paiute people, the attack on the Salish, and that had twice attacked Gabe and Ezra, was sufficient motivation to track him down and exact retribution.

"You should see yourself," chuckled Ezra as he rode beside Gabe. He glanced at his friend, shook his head and laughed. "That hat, you've got it cockeyed, if I didn't know better I'd think you were tryin' to look like a pirate! All you need is a black patch over one eye!"

Gabe chuckled, "Aye matey! An' if you don't mind y'self, I'll be makin' ye walk the plank!"

They had just rounded the point of the long ridge of mountains that sided the west edge of the valley and now faced the broad plains of the Snake River. The flat land plains were a two days ride wide, north and south, and ten days or more east to west. The Snake River flowed west through the middle of the flats before turning north to eventually join the Columbia in the reaches of the far north. Gabe had no idea of the location of the Waiilatpus, but the tracks showed their prey was hugging the southern tips of the Bitterroot Mountains and moving basically southwest.

Once in the open, Gabe kicked Ebony to a canter, anxious to catch up to the thief and not wanting to risk losing him to the terrain or the elements or his own subterfuge. The horses stretched out, eager to cover the ground before them. Gabe and Ezra leaned into the wind, easily following the trail of the lone rider before them. The dry topsoil had been kicked up by the fleeing Tauitau, but it was evident he was moving at a trot or a walk most of the time. When a horse stretches to a canter or gallop, the length of the stride and the spacing of the hoofprints varies more than a walk or a trot. These were close, evenly spaced, and the men were anxious to close the gap.

The day was clear, the azure sky free of clouds and the afternoon sun warmed the shoulders of the riders. Gabe soon reined Ebony back to a trot, then to a walk, letting the big stallion catch his wind. The other animals were starting to lather, the intermittent breeze doing little to cool them. Another long ridge of mountains that paralleled the first, pushed into the flats. The greenery of the valley between the ridges faded from view as they neared a thicket of juniper with a pair of tall ponderosa lifting their heads high above, and Gabe motioned to Ezra to go to the trees. A little oasis of aspen surrounded a trickle of water that came from a spring and offered ample water for the horses and mule. The men let them drink as they loosened the girths and as the horses turned to the low-growing grass nearby, the men allowed a few minutes for the water to clear, then went to one knee to scoop handfuls of water to their mouths. Ezra sat back on his haunches, "That's some mighty refreshing water, cold, clear, ummm."

"It is that. And you notice the tracks of that back-stabber haven't stopped yet. His horse is gonna give out soon," answered Gabe.

"And it don't make sense! Most natives we've known have been almighty careful with their horses and take better care of 'em than most others, but this'ns actin' like . . . I dunno what."

"You don't suppose he knows we're after him?"

"Nah, he was gone long 'fore we took out. But he might just assume we'd be on his trail."

"Why? We didn't trail after him when he and the other'n hit our camp, so why would he think it this time?" questioned Gabe.

"Whatever is pushin' him, he's goin' pretty much in a straight line southwest, stayin' just away from these foothills," countered Ezra, nodding to the hills on their right that held the thick timber.

"I'm thinkin' we need to pace the horses, but we have to do what we can to catch up with him, 'fore he gets to his village or people."

"So, what'chu thinkin'?"

"We'll stretch 'em out until dusk, stop for some food and such, let 'em catch their wind and rest up. The moon'll still be full, rises early this time of year, and we can trail him by moonlight."

Ezra grinned, "Figgered as much," he answered, taking another bite from the pemmican.

Another ten miles and they moved across the mouth
of another valley that lay between mountain ridges.
But what was of more concern was the extensive
lava field that blocked their way. The tracks of the
Waiilatpus warrior turned toward the mouth of the
valley and took to a narrow trail that penetrated the
sagebrush and shouldered the lava field. Dusk was
threatening to lower the curtain on the day as they
broke from the sage, spotted a knoll with greenery
on the back side and the men agreed to stop.

They stripped the gear from the horses and mule,
rubbed them down with dry grass and let them roll
and start to graze. There was no running water, but
Ezra started looking around for a possible tank in
the rocks, a depression that might have caught some
rainwater, the shade keeping it from evaporating,
maybe enough for the animals.

Gabe said, "I'm gonna climb this butte, take a look
'n see if I can find any sign of that man's camp. Surely
he has to stop, but I doubt if we'll see any fire, but I'm
gonna look anyway."

"Alright, I'm gonna see if I can find some water for
the horses."

The men nodded to one another as they parted,
and Gabe started his climb up the knoll. Wolf trotted
beside him, as they leaned into the climb, choosing to
angle up the long slope to the crest. Gabe struggled,

the twisted ankle sending stabbing pain up his leg and making him favor the downhill foot. Every step reminded him of each of his injuries, the sweat at the band of his hat beginning to trail down his face, the salt burning his wound. He shook his head, put one foot before the other, and forced himself to move.

Once atop, Gabe quickly dropped to seat himself, legs outstretched, and knees bent as he uncased the scope. The entire flat to his left was covered with black lava, while to the south the foothills pushed away the lava and the well-traveled trail bent around the point. As he slowly moved the scope to scan the trail, he searched for any glimmer of light, knowing that even the smallest fire could be seen for miles, even the glow of one can be a giveaway to an observant watcher. Yet he searched, and the more he saw, the more certain he was the man they pursued did not know they were following, there had been no attempt to obscure his tracks, and he made no deviation on his direction. *He either believes he's not followed, or he's not concerned. Perhaps he's focused on his destination and his great coup and score of the rifle.* Just the thought of his rifle stirred his anger, but he would not surrender to the emotion that could warp his judgement.

He sat up and stretched out his legs, resting his swollen ankle, and absorbing the cooling air that came with the dropping of the sun below the mountains. Even here in the foothills, once the sun was down, the temperature would drop, and it was getting late in the summer. He had known it to snow in the high mountains even this early, but he did not believe that snow was in the offing, but cooler weather seemed to be moving close. He searched the broad vista without the scope, squinting slightly at any indication of light, but still he saw nothing. He started to lift the scope again, and paused, looking directly ahead at the base of a finger ridge that pushed against the lava field. There, at the point, where the trail parted two smaller lava fields and at the end of the ridge, the reflected glow of a fire. He lifted the scope, saw only the glare, but he knew he was not mistaken, and that had to be their quarry.

He judged the distance right at five miles, but with tired horses, it might as well be fifty miles. Yet if the man stayed there for the night, they could overtake him as they traveled by moonlight. Gabe grinned as he scanned the area again with the scope, then lowered it and rubbed Wolf's scruff, and stood, just as a distant howl of another wolf lifted into the dim light of dusk. The cry rose, leveled for an instant, then trailed off to a couple of barks, then fell silent. Wolf had stopped and looked in the direction of the cry, glanced at Gabe, then lifted his head to the first stars of the evening, and sent his answering cry into the darkness.

Gabe grinned and started down, but another howl came, and Wolf stopped, watched Gabe move away, then lifted his head to answer again. Gabe paused, said, "You do what you want boy, it's alright." And turned away to descend the hillside, limping as he tenderly took each step. He glanced back, but Wolf was gone. Gabe shook his head and whispered, "Hope you find her, but whoever it is, don't forget to come back Wolf."

Their camp was in the trees, in a basin that shielded them from every direction but where they came from, and Ezra was certain their hat sized fire would not be seen by anyone that wasn't within ten yards of their camp, even the glow of the fire was shielded by the thick trees. Gabe walked into the camp, smelled the coffee and grinned, "That smells mighty good!" he declared as he seated himself on a grey log near the fire.

Ezra could tell by his expression there was something good about what he saw and he asked, "Alright, what'd ya' see?"

"I'm pretty sure I spotted his camp, the glow of a fire anyway. Too small for a hunting party and wouldn't be seen except from up high and with a scope, so whoever it is, won't know he's been seen."

"How far?" asked Ezra, pouring the coffee for both. He handed the cup to Gabe, sat down on a rock opposite and sipped the sizzling hot brew as he waited.

"Bout five miles."

Ezra grinned as he lowered the cup, glanced at his friend and nodded, knowing what would come next.

27 / CLASH

The lanterns of the night shone brightly above, the moon added a touch of silver to the land and the men saddled up and loaded the pack animals and stepped out quietly into the glimmering night. They stayed off the trail, the horses' hooves padding in the soft soil as they pointed due south. The shoulder of the ridge stood before them and the rakish shadow pointed to the lava flats and the black void. Gabe focused on the shoulder, sighting their path in a direct line, letting Ebony have his head and the animals, now rested, stepped lightly. The men had cleaned and reloaded each of their weapons, and Gabe had the strung Mongol bow hung at his back, the quiver of arrows by his right hip, as always, secured with the long tie down by the cantle.

Gabe remembered what he saw with the scope and knew there were two finger ridges, one before

the other, and his plan was to leave the horses behind the first ridge and make their approach on foot.
Within about a half hour, they were riding into the
shadow of the first and smaller ridge that held a
smattering of piñon on the lee side that they would
use to shelter the horses.

A slight depression on the slope of the ridge was
thick with trees and brush, the site chosen for the
horses and as they stepped down, they noticed an old
trail, probably made by the ancients, that had broken
the edge of the slope and offered a way around the
point. The sage was thick and shoulder high, offering
ample cover and Gabe led the way as they moved
away from the trail. He held the bow with a nocked
arrow at his side, picking his steps through the brush
and cacti, when the yip, yip, yip of a coyote lifted
from somewhere in the flats. Gabe froze, his foot
almost to fall, when an answering howl came from
less than ten yards away, and atop a bit of shoulder of
the ridge point. He breathed easy, knowing the night
song of the coyotes would give the fugitive warrior
a sense of security. He waited a moment longer, and
moved slowly ahead, staying in the shadows of the
sage, never a sound. He sensed, rather than knew,
Ezra was behind him for the man was as stealthy as
a barn cat after a mouse.

They dropped into a crouch as they neared the spot
where Gabe had seen the fire, listening, watching, but

nothing moved and no sound came. There was not the swishing of the tail of a horse, no slight grunt when a horse would shift its weight. No sound of snoring or heavy breathing of a man, but there was also no sound of the ever-present cicadas, crickets, or night hawks. No scurrying jackrabbits, lizards, or foxes. Nothing. Gabe froze in place, going to one knee, peering into the night shadows, but there was nothing. His breathing was shallow, his chest slowly rising and falling, only his eyes moved. He waited.

Behind them the massive lava field stood like a ten foot tall barrier that stretched hundreds of yards in both directions, the black lava had absorbed the heat of the day and now, cooling in the night air, crackled and groaned like a monstrous dragon coming awake. Even though the air was cool, Gabe felt sweat trickle down between his shoulder blades and he fought against movement, knowing the slightest twitch could give him away and bring death knocking. He heard a swish, looked up to see something squirming as it flew through the air toward them, and he realized, *RATTLESNAKE!!!*

Gabe hunkered down, heard Ezra moving in the brush and heard the twisting serpent land in the tall sagebrush, no more than ten feet away. He knew the warrior had taken a trick from their playbook. Gabe squinted his eyes, searching the brush for the snake when an arrow whispered past his shoulder.

He dropped to the ground, hissed to Ezra, "He spotted us, move!" and with all fours he scampered away from the snake and toward the shooter. He went to his belly under a wide spreading sage, fearing to breathe, and listened. He waited, then heard the soft brush of buckskin against a branch, coming closer. He lifted himself to one knee, brought his bow to full draw and waited. A shadow moved, but it was too close in the vicinity to Ezra, then the swish of the war club crashed through the sage and struck. A groan as the man dropped, but then the shuffling of feet as he scrambled out of reach of Ezra's club. Gabe looked into the darkness, detected movement and sent an arrow whispering through the tall brush.

Gabe instantly nocked another arrow, held still, listening and waiting. But the man had either stopped or was not injured enough to hinder his movements any further and he moved silently. Gabe felt Ezra near, a whisper from behind asked, "Where?"

Gabe nodded toward the last position he knew the man to be, and a scream came almost from behind them as the man launched himself over the sage, for an instant silhouetted in the moonlight as he flew like an ogre, arms outstretched, a knife in one hand a war hawk in the other. Gabe moved one way, Ezra the other and the screaming attacker slapped his hawk against the side of Ezra's head as he swiped at Gabe's leaning form with the knife. Ezra stumbled backwards, dazed as he saw stars where there were none, and staggered against the prickly brush. Gabe spun toward the man who rolled as he fell coming up and twisting around to face Gabe, snarling, and spitting like an angry catamount.

Gabe stepped back, the Mongol bow held before him and as the man readied his attack, he brought the bow to full draw and loosed the arrow at the attacker. The man ducked to the side, the arrow sliced through the muscle at his shoulder and the man screamed. He glared at Gabe, his eyes appearing like the fire orange he had seen in Wolf's eyes when he was attacking, then lunged toward the white man. Gabe tossed aside his bow, and snatched his hawk with his right hand, his knife with his left, and twisted his body as the attacker stumbled past. Gabe spun to face the maniac of the night, saw the moonlight bounce off the sweaty back and the man hunkered, arms wide. The space among the tall sage was less than a typical room, irregular shaped because of the big sage and intermittent greasewood and bunch grass, yet the moon moved away from the clouds and shone bright, illuminating the combatants as they circled one another.

Tauitau feinted with the knife, Gabe did not flinch. Tauitau lunged with the knife, edge up, as he lifted his hawk to distract Gabe's attention, but Gabe stepped and twisted aside as the knife came forward, then slashed down with his own knife, drawing blood across the bicep of Tauitau. The man winced, withdrew quickly and glanced at his wound. He spat, snarled as he lifted one corner of his lip and glared at Gabe with hatred burning in his eyes. Gabe grinned, chuckled, and stood nonchalantly, shaking his head. He watched as the Waiilatpus warrior, breathing heavily, glared and shifted his weight side to side. Gabe saw blood dripping from the side of the man's head, probably from the blow of Ezra's warclub, and his upper right arm was covered with blood.

Gabe spoke in Shoshone, "If you return my rifle, we'll let you live and return to your people!"

The man's eyes showed recognition, and he cocked his head to the side, "You are not Shoshone!" Tauitau had learned to speak the language of the enemies of his people and had led his warriors against the Northern Shoshone many times, taking horses and captives and bounty.

Gabe grinned again, "We are friends with the Shoshone and have wives from the Shoshone. We are friends with many people, the Salish, and the Paiute that you fought! You and your cowardly warriors destroyed a village of the Paiute, then turned your tails and ran when you tried again!"

Tauitau screamed and charged, hawk lifted, and knife held low. He took three steps and the warclub of Ezra whistled through the dim moonlight and collided with the man's shoulder and neck, knocking him to the ground. Gabe and Ezra both rushed to the downed figure, ready to strike another blow, but he was unconscious and lay in a heap. Ezra picked up the man's knife and hawk, stuffed them into his belt and said, "Let's see if we can find his camp, get your rifle."

Gabe took a deep breath that lifted his shoulders as he looked down at the man. "He's a mean one, think we oughta tie him up or somethin'?"

"Nah, he'll be out for a spell, we can leave him be, get your rifle and get gone. No need to kill when we don't have to, ya reckon?"

"I reckon," shrugged Gabe and bent to pick up his bow and follow Ezra out of the sage. The semblance of a camp was found only because the man's horse was tethered to a low clump of greasewood. No other sign showed where the man had camped. "He musta covered over his fire, done a good job of it too," observed Gabe as he walked toward the man's horse. In a heap beside the animal was Tauitau's blanket, his bow and quiver and when Gabe toed the blanket, he saw the butt of the Ferguson. He grinned as he bent to retrieve his weapon, was pleased to see no obvious damage, and snapped open the frizzen to see it was empty. He nodded, snapped it shut, and cradled the rifle in his arm, his bow across his back, and looked at Ezra with a wide grin. "Got it!"

"Then let's get outta this place, it gives me the hee-biejeebs!" as he pointed to the lava fields with its odd formations and black foreboding flats.

They returned to their horses, and Gabe, now mounted, frowned, heard what he was certain was the distant thunder of hooves and grinned, "I think our friend came to and took off!"

Ezra frowned, listened and heard the diminishing sounds of a running horse, then nodded. "Maybe we shoulda killed him, I'd hate to think of him gettin' up a war party and comin' after us again!"

"For a minute there, I thought you had killed him. That war club smacked him mighty hard, sounded like you hit a hollow tree trunk."

"If it hadn't hit his shoulder first, I think it woulda killed him. I swung it flat so the blade wouldn't take his head off . . . gets too bloody that way."

Gabe shook his head as he reined his big black around to start their journey home. They had gone less than a mile when a shadowy figure of a black wolf came trotting from the side slope of a nearby foothill and trotted alongside. "Welcome back boy. Was she pretty?"

Wolf, tongue lolling to the side, looked over his shoulder at the man as if to say, "Of course."

28 / CAMP

It was nearing the end of the second day after re-covering the rifle that they rounded the point at the mouth of the valley of the buffalo hunt. The camp of the Salish was still there and as the sun nestled atop the western peaks, Gabe and Ezra rode into camp, trailing their pack animals and looking a little wea-ry. Spotted Eagle had been told of their coming and walked to greet his friends. As they approached, Eagle lifted his hand in welcome and Gabe and Ezra slid to the ground. Their horses' heads hung low, and they stood, tired and dusty.

Eagle greeted, "I see you have your rifle. Did you take your vengeance on the Waiilatpus?"

Gabe grinned, "We tussled a bit, left him in the brush, but he was still alive."

Eagle frowned, "You should have killed him! He will come for vengeance upon you! It is the way of his people!"

"Well, I had my rifle and he lit out like his horse's tail was on fire and I just didn't feel like givin' chase. So, if he comes back for more," he glanced to Ezra, "we'll just have to deal him another hand."

Eagle shook his head, took a deep breath that lifted his shoulders, and turned to lead the men to their camp site. As Gabe walked beside him, Eagle said, "We will leave at first light. My woman and others have prepared your meat, smoked, cured, bundled it in the hides. It is beside my lodge."

"We're mighty grateful to you and the women for doin' that for us, Eagle. We'll be there 'fore first light and load it on our pack animals." They walked a short distance before Gabe asked, "You goin' back the way you came, that trail beyond those mountains yonder?"

"Yes. It is wide and easy traveling for the travois." He turned to look at his friend, "Will you ride with us?"

"We're kinda anxious to get back to our women folk and we'll take that trail in the valley below. It's a good 'un, and we can do it with the loaded packers. It cuts a day or so off the travel."

"It is good," replied Eagle. They had come to the camp at the edge of the trees where they had slept before and Eagle turned to leave. He paused, looked back at his friend, "You told me you would speak of your God when I was ready. When you have eaten, I will return and we will talk."

Gabe nodded, glanced to Ezra and said to Eagle, "That will be good, Eagle. We'll wait for you."

The moon was waning from full but still showed three quarters and was bright on this starlit night. The air was cool, and the valley slumbered as Spotted Eagle and his woman, Prairie Flower, walked into the circle of light by the small campfire of Gabe and Ezra. "Welcome folks, would you like some coffee?"

Eagle grinned, nodded, glanced at his woman who frowned and said, "I have not had this, coffee."

"Then we'll just get you a cup and let you try it." He nodded to Ezra, "Might wanna get some sugar for the lady." Ezra grinned and went to the packs to fetch some sweetener.

Gabe poured the two spare cups full, stretched out with one cup for Ezra to put in some sugar, then handed it to Prairie Flower and the other to Eagle. They were seated on the long grey log that had at one time been a proud ponderosa but had probably been a victim of a blowdown across the valley. Such happenings were common in the mountains and usually left a tangle of downed trees and branches that made movement through the woods difficult.

Gabe and Ezra were seated on a stump and a rock respectively and sipped at their own coffee as they watched Flower timidly taste the black brew. She sipped, frowned as she looked at the coffee, sipped again and smiled as she smacked her lips and asked, "Is that the coffee or that powder you put in?"

"A little of both. The coffee takes a little gettin' used to, and the sugar kinda helps take the edge off," responded Gabe.

She looked at Eagle's cup, "Let me taste it without the sugar." He handed her the cup, let her sip at it, frown and shake her head. "It is better with the sugar!" and hugged the cup close to her breast.

The men chuckled, and Gabe looked at Eagle, "I s'pose Red Hawk has talked to you some while we've been gone, about what he learned, I mean."

"Yes, but it is not the way of my people for the father to learn from the son, that is why I spoke to you."

Gabe nodded, glanced to Ezra then back to Eagle, "I've heard you mention the Creator, so how 'bout you telling me about what you and your people believe about the Creator."

Eagle squirmed a little, looked to Flower and began, "The stories told by the elders are the way we pass on the beliefs and the past events of our people. The story of the Creator began when he made all the animals. The first one was Coyote, and he was sent before the others and before man because throughout the world was evil and Coyote, and his brother, Fox were to remove the evil. He also made many things of the world, the mountains, and lakes and more. He also made many good things, skills, and wisdom, for man. But he left some bad things like anger, hunger, greed, and others. Since that time Coyote has been known as a trickster." He paused, took a long sip of coffee, sat the cup down and leaned forward with his elbows on his knees and continued.

"When a young man is considered old enough, he will go on a vision quest or a vigil to seek his spirit-guide to help him overcome the evils left by Coyote. Sometimes the Shaman will aid the young man in that quest and help him find his guide. Every winter, our people will have a guardian spirit dance, with dances, feasts, and prayers. It is one of the most important times in a young person's life, for it is the spirit guide that will be with him the rest of his life." He stopped, lifted the coffee cup toward Gabe for a refill and waited.

Gabe reached for his Bible and opened it to the first page, looked up at Eagle and Flower, then nodded toward the Bible, "This book and these writings were given to us by the Creator. The words begin here," he pointed to the page and began, "*In the beginning, God created the heaven,*" he pointed to the stars above, "*and the earth,*" sweeping his hand across the land below them. "*And the earth was without form, and void; and darkness was upon the face of the deep. And the Spirit of God moved upon the face of the waters. And God said, Let there be light: and there was light.*" He paused, looked at Eagle, lifted the Bible, "This book tells about everything, how God created the animals, fish, trees, everything, and then He created man."

Gabe scooted a little closer, "And like you said about evil, yes there was evil, but God did not want that and knew that evil kept us from knowing Him. He calls it sin and tells us that all of us have sinned and because of that sin, what we deserve is Hell forever, and He tells us about that Hell. It is a burning pit that those that do not know God are cast into and burn forever." Gabe paused, dropped his eyes and drew a deep breath, looked up at Eagle again and said, "But God loves us, and does not want us to face that penalty. So he tells us here," and he turned toward the back of the Bible and flipped through the pages, pointed at Romans 6:23, "*For the wages of sin,*" he paused and explained, "sin is the evil that we do, '*is death: but the gift of God is eternal life through Jesus Christ our Lord.*'"

Gabe saw the frown on Eagle's face and continued. "Let me explain a bit," he flipped back a couple pages and pointed to Romans 5:12 *"Wherefore, as by one man sin entered into the world, and death by sin; and so death passed upon all men for that all have sinned.'* But remember, He said that there was a gift of eternal life. That's because here," and he pointed to verse 8 of chapter 5, "*But God commendeth,* or showed, *his love toward us in that while we were yet sinners, Christ died for us.*" He scooted closer still, elbows on his knees and said, "There is evil in the world and we do that evil, and God says the price we have to pay is death, or hell forever, but He also made a way out. He sent His son, Jesus, to pay that price for us, and like the verse said, *'the gift of God is eternal life through Jesus Christ our Lord.'"*

Gabe looked from Eagle to Flower, saw both were very focused on what was being said and he asked, "Do you understand this, that He offers each of us a free gift of eternal life?"

Eagle frowned, "Does that mean we live forever and never die?"

Gabe grinned, "No, everyone dies, but like your people believe, the spirit of a man still lives. But without the gift of eternal life, our spirit will not live in Heaven."

"But we believe that our spirit will cross over, there!" and he pointed to the Milky Way that stretched high above.

Gabe nodded, "Many peoples, like your people, have a similar belief. That is why God has given us this book, to bring you and the others the answer. God wants you to know for sure that Heaven is your home and He wants you to have the power of the Holy Spirit to guide you. That happens when you accept His free gift of eternal life He tells about here." He pointed to the verse in Romans.

Eagle frowned, thinking, and glanced at his woman, Prairie Flower. She sat beside him, quiet but with a pleasant expression on her face and her eyes wide as she let a bit of a smile paint her face. Eagle looked back to Gabe, "How do we get this gift?"

Gabe looked down at the Bible, flipped a couple pages and pointed at Romans 10:9 and read, *"That if thou shalt confess with thy mouth the Lord Jesus, and shalt believe in thine heart that God hath raised him from the dead, thou shalt be saved."* Then he moved his finger down to verse 13, *"For whosoever shall call upon the name of the Lord shall be saved."*

"What does it mean 'be saved'?" asked Flower.

"To be saved from that penalty for sin, death and hell forever. When you pray and accept his gift of eternal life, He saves you from that penalty. That is 'to be saved'."

"Will you show us how to do this?" asked Flower, glancing to Eagle who gave a slight nod.

"Yes, we can do that now, if you wish," answered Gabe. Both Eagle and Flower nodded, and Gabe bowed his head and began praying. As he prayed he cautioned them, "Don't do this unless you mean it with your heart," and continued and led them in a simple prayer to ask forgiveness for their sin and to ask for the gift of eternal life. Both repeated the prayer as Gabe suggested, and when the prayer was done, all said, "Amen."

Eagle lifted his eyes, smiling broadly, and said to his friend, "It is good to do this. Is this what my son and the other young people learned when they were with you?"

"Yes, and they learned even more. Your son, Red Hawk, learned to understand these markings," he pointed to the pages of the Bible, "and I want you to take this and let your son teach you how to know these markings and you can learn much more about our God and Creator."

Eagle smiled, cautiously accepted the great gift offered by his friend, and Gabe saw a tear well up in the man's eye, but Eagle quickly wiped it away as he reached for the Bible. He held it close to his chest and looked to Flower and Ezra and back to Gabe, "You are a great friend." The four embraced one another and parted, each one full of thoughts for the coming days and even further. It was a good night.

29 / RETURN

With an early start they were passing the point of the buffalo kill by late morning. Their chosen trail would take them almost to the head of the valley before they took the cut to the north and into the mountains that bordered the north edge, but it would be more than a day's travel to the cut. By the end of the second day out from the Salish camp, they made the cut from the valley and crested a low pass that dropped into a long valley pointing north. The sun was dropping behind the western peaks when they went to camp at the foot of the pass where the north slope of a hillside was covered with aspen and a bottom of the draw held a little spring. They were anxious to be home and had pushed the horses hard the first two days, but now stripped the gear, rubbed them down and let them take water from the spring and graze on some deep grass at the edge of the trees. Once the animals were tethered, Gabe stood, turned to look at the sky in the twilight and slapped his shoulders, "Brrr! It's gettin' cold mighty early, don'tcha think?"

"I been noticin' that. Looky there," suggested Ezra, pointing at the upper end of the aspen. "Showin' gold already. I be thinkin' we're gonna have an early and hard winter."

"It does seem a mite early. What is it, late August, early September?"

Ezra chuckled, slapped his pockets and the chest of his tunic where there were no pockets, and with a shrug and an innocent look to his friend, answered, "Dunno, can't seem to find my calendar!"

Gabe turned away, grumbling, and trying not to laugh at the antics of his friend. He stooped to pick up some dead wood, shed branches from the aspen, and went to the flat beside the little spring fed creek and dropped the bundle, then went back to the stand of trees to gather some more. When he returned, Ezra was already blowing on the tinder to bring the spark to life and fanned the beginning of flame that licked at the kindling. While he nursed the fire, Gabe picked up the coffeepot and went to the spring for fresh water.

Ezra cut some steaks from the loin of the buffalo, hung them over the fire on green branches, and pushed aside some coals to drop the camas bulbs into the ashes. He sat back and waited for the water to start boiling so they could drop in the coffee that Gabe was busy grinding on the boulder nearby. The breeze was steady but seemed to be growing colder as the dusk began to fade and darkness threatened. Ezra looked at Gabe, "Think we need to build a lean-to tonite?"

"Why, you thinkin' snow?"

"It's gettin' cold enough, might be an early one."

"Nah, it ain't gonna snow, maybe get colder, but no snow."

Ezra made a face that showed skepticism with uplifted eyebrows, but he shrugged and answered the call of the coffeepot as it started dancing beside the fire. He motioned to Gabe to bring the coffee and the pot was soon sending the mouth-watering smell of coffee into the camp. It was just a short while until the steaks and camas was ready and the two friends were soon enjoying their high-country repast. Wolf lay at the feet of Gabe, catching the trimming off the steak and waiting for more, but none were forth-coming. He stood and trotted into the trees, as Gabe said, "Guess he's goin' to look for his own supper, or maybe his girlfriend."

"Ya never know 'bout them lone wolves, especially them husky, good-lookin' ones!"

Both men chuckled, Gabe shook his head as he poured some more coffee to top off his meal. He sat the cup aside, took the plates and utensils and went to the pool below the spring to wash things in the cold water, using the sandy soil for the scrubbing.

He wiped his hands on his buckskin britches and returned to the camp to put the dishes in the parfleche that rode behind the panniers that carried the buffalo meat. All the meat had been de-boned, hung to dry and was smoked overnight by the women at the Salish camp, the bigger cuts had a thin bark on the outside, one pannier held nothing but the many strips of smoked meat, the other the bigger cuts. The two panniers carried by the mule were loaded in a similar fashion and there were two large pieces cut from the hind quarters, tied and bundled, that had also been smoked to form the bark to preserve, and would ride atop the pack saddles, but for now were hung from a high branch on a big aspen. When they were on the trail, the packs were covered with the hides of the two buffalo, but the men chose to use the hides for ground cover for their bedrolls.

The long day riding demanded they turn to their bedrolls early and neither man protested, although Gabe did stoke up the fire a mite, lay a few bigger pieces of firewood within reach, before he slipped under the covers. Ezra was across the fire from him and grunted his approval as he pulled his blanket over his shoulder. Wolf returned and lay against Gabe on the far side, away from the fire and Gabe grinned into the darkness, knowing he would be snug and warm on this cold night. He lay on his back, hands behind his head, as he looked at the dark sky, watching the stars light their lanterns for the night, and thought about the many nights they had spent on the ground, under the open sky, and enjoying the freedom of the wilderness.

The low growl that came from Wolf well after midnight, went unheard by Gabe who had the blanket over his face and ears, his floppy hat pulled down, and was sleeping contentedly. Wolf rose slowly to his feet and moved away from Gabe's side, padding his way to the edge of the trees. The horses were tethered on the far side, behind Ezra, and Wolf moved on the downhill side toward the little creek. He glanced over his shoulder at the sleeping men, then moved further into the trees.

About an hour later, Wolf padded back to the side of his friend and stretched out beside him, dropping his chin between his paws. He lifted his head to look back at the trees, glanced at the fire and listened to its sporadic hissing, then turned back and lay still, slipping into a comforting snooze. He whimpered once, because of a dream or remembering what he had done, and lay still again.

"Not gonna snow, huh!? Then what's all this white stuff?!" growled Ezra, flipping back his blanket and struggling to his feet. He grumbled some more as he grabbed at the firewood and stirred up the coals, surprised to find some still glowing under the grey ashes and melted snow. Within moments he had flames licking at the firewood, and his hands outstretched for warmth. He had brushed off the flat rock used for grinding the coffee and pulled it closer to the fire, as he snarled at Gabe, "You gonna sleep all day or you gonna build a snowman?"

Gabe groaned, mumbled something under the blankets and flipped back the covers to peer about, "Well, whaddya know, it did snow!" He grinned as he carefully flipped the rest of his blanket back, then stood and stretched. "My, it's a beautiful morning!" He looked around, frowned and walked toward the stack of gear, "Oh oh," he said, as he bent down to look at a parfleche that had been dumped out and cast aside. He stood, looked at the tracks, looked at Wolf who lay with head down between his paws and looking at Gabe out of the corner of his eyes, his ears drooping.

"Don't tell me Wolf got into it?" asked Ezra.

"Nope, but he didn't do anything about it either!" He cocked his head to the side and looked at the recalcitrant canine as he looked away to ignore Gabe.

Ezra stood and walked closer, looking at the tracks all about the gear. Although slightly smudged by the fresh snowfall, it was evident the thief in the night had done his deed after it started snowing and left before it quit. Ezra frowned, bent down, and fanned the fresh snow from a track, looked up at Gabe and said, "It was a bear!"

"Ummhmm, and Wolf was with him. Look there!" he pointed to the edge of the gear at a jumble of tracks.

Ezra walked to the gear, went to a knee, and once again fanned away the fresh snow, and there, side by side, were the tracks of a big wolf and a yearling bear. He looked up at Gabe, "Looks like they were playin' together!" He shook his head, stood, and added, "And my momma always said, 'Don't play at the supper table!'"

Gabe couldn't help but chuckle, then shook his head, pointed to Wolf with his chin, "And look at him. He knows what he did and he's not the least bit sorry!"

"And one thing for sure, you can't give a hundred-fifty-pound wild wolf a spanking!"

"Ain't that the truth. But he knows we're not happy," nodding toward the wolf who still would not look at them.

Gabe looked at the dim grey line in the east, "Guess we might as well get a move on, if we can't get home by nightfall, we can at least get close enough so we can get there 'fore noon tomorrow."

And it was a long day that ended when they made camp by the light of the moon amidst the long shadows of towering ponderosa. They had made it into the flat-bottomed canyon bordered by black forest and wound its way to eventually open into the wide flats they called home. But it was too far to try to make it

with tired horses and weary riders. Tomorrow would
be soon enough, and they should be there by mid-day,
or a little sooner, if they got another early start. As
they turned in, Wolf came to Gabe's side and was cautioned, "Now, no playin' with the bears tonight!" as he
gave the black wolf a stern expression and shook his
finger at him. Wolf's ears hung limply, and he lowered
his head as he looked at Gabe with sorrowful eyes,
at least until Gabe ran his fingers through the scruff
of his neck and Wolf smiled, with an open mouth
and lolling tongue and wagging tail. Gabe chuckled
and slipped into his blankets as Wolf lay beside him.
Tomorrow, they should be home.

30 / HOME

The rising sun was stretching long shadows toward the cabin as Cougar Woman and Grey Dove, busy with the little ones, were getting ready to go to the valley and lake below the cabin to gather the last of the huckleberries as they hung heavy on the bushes near the lake. Cougar bundled the little boy, Bobcat, into the cradle board as Dove did the same with her little girl, Squirrel. Dove's older boy, Chipmunk, sat on the floor, watching his mother fuss with the cover for the cradle board as he chewed on the biscuit from his breakfast. Chipmunk was pushing two years old and was a busy toddler, very little slowed down the curious and strong-willed boy.

Dove looked at Cougar Woman, "Are we taking our rifles?"

"You can take yours; I will take my bow, but if we get the parfleches full, they will be enough to carry."

"With that dusting of snow, the berries will be sweet and ready. But you know they attract bears also," declared Dove.

"And if one comes along, his fat will be good for our winter stores," asserted a smiling Cougar.

"Have you ever taken a bear with your bow?" asked Dove, looking at her friend with a bit of a cock to her head and eyes squinted a mite.

"I have not, but I can," suggested a grinning Cougar Woman.

They helped one another lift the cradleboards with the little ones to their backs and once they were settled and secure, Dove took Chipmunk's hand and the women left the cabin. It was an easy walk down to the lake in the valley, the trail simple to follow and the little bit of snow had already melted, showing white only in the shade of the thicker trees and on a few branches of the leafy aspen. They walked together, enjoying the stretch of the legs and time together and out of the cabin. The children had kept them in or close to the cabin for several days and they sought the time away and in the open.

As they came from the trees and the valley opened before them, they stopped to enjoy the beauty of the golden blanket that lay upon the tall bushes and willows that dotted the valley floor. The rising sun gave the hint of autumn's color to the green carpeted valley, that would soon show a palette of colors from the red of the oak brush, to the orange and gold of the aspen. "The season of color is coming soon," declared Cougar, nodding to the upper end of the valley and the touches of color that showed where lighter green told of thick aspen groves.

"When it comes early, it brings a long hard winter," suggested Grey Dove.

"Yes, and we must be prepared. When the men return with the buffalo, there will be much to do, perhaps a hunt or two for more meat."

They walked down the slight shoulder with the scattered oak brush and moved along the west bank of the lake. Most of the berry bushes were in a long line that followed the far end of the west bank and even from this distance, they could be seen with humble branches heavy with fruit. The women glanced at one another, smiling because of the anticipated harvest. The berries could be used for many things, flavoring for pemmican, added to the batter for biscuits, and dried to be used during the long winter months. The heavy dark colored berry was also used for tea and as a pain-relieving medicine.

When they drew near the bushes, Dove stopped and lifted off the cradle board, leaned it against the large boulder that sat between the lake shore and the brush, then leaned her rifle beside it. She arched her back to stretch the muscles, already sore from the short walk, and watched as Chipmunk toddled about, exploring the grass that grew knee deep on him, and the edge of the bushes. He plucked a tiny handful of the dark berries, put one in his mouth, and made a face at the slightly bitter taste, but continued chewing and swallowed the treat.

Cougar Woman sat her bow and quiver next to Dove's rifle, stood the cradle board with Bobcat next to Squirrel's, and stepped back. She noticed some red near the boulder, bent and plucked a handful of ripe raspberries and popped one in her mouth, handing some to Dove. She smiled at the sweet taste of the ripe fruit and offered one to Chipmunk as he toddled near. The boy gladly accepted and put it in his mouth, chewed quickly and swallowed, and extended a pudgy hand for more.

Dove chuckled, "He's just like his father, always hungry!"

Cougar Woman laughed, agreeing with her friend, then suggested, "If you want to gather the berries near here to watch the little ones, I will start over there," pointing to the far edge, "and work back to here."

"That is good, I must nurse Squirrel before I start," explained Dove, reaching for her cradleboard with the infant, Squirrel.

Cougar smiled, and nodded, reached for her bow and quiver and the small parfleche. She walked along the shore, working her way to the far edge of the brush. The meandering creek that came from the high mountains and fed the lake, had cut a wide swath through the grassy flats that separated the lake brush from the trees on the long ridge that bordered the west edge of the valley. The thicket of berry bushes skirted a slight knoll that was freckled with twisted cedar, juniper, and piñon. A shore hugging band of about thirty feet wide was nothing but huckleberry bushes.

Cougar rounded the point, looked around the flat stretch between the thick trees and the brush, then searched the bushes for the heaviest fruit. She smiled as she spotted one that appeared thick with berries and started her harvesting. Carefully grasping a thick cluster, she gently pulled it from the branch, dropped it into the parfleche, and reached for another. She was focused on her work and slowly started through the bush in the general direction of Dove.

Having finished her nursing, Dove secured Squirrel in her cradleboard, noted Bobcat was snoozing, and as she finished adjusting her tunic, she spoke to Chipmunk. "We will pick some berries here," nodding to the heavy bushes as she stood, slipped the rifle sling over her shoulder, and picked up her parfleche to begin. Chipmunk followed in his mother's steps, occasionally picking a few berries, and dropping every other one into the parfleche, mimicking his mother. Dove glanced at the sun that shone brightly as it stood above the eastern ridge. She looked at the western ridge, thick with black timber and saw the big lowering moon, hanging resolutely in the pale blue morning sky, just above the western horizon. It would soon bow to the brighter sun and tuck itself away until darkness beckoned once again.

It was late morning when Cougar neared the edge of the bushes, and heard little Bobcat whimpering, probably expressing his hunger. She pushed through the brush to find Dove returning to their point of beginning, Chipmunk holding to the fringe at her leggings, and a heavy parfleche at her side. The women compared their harvest, jabbering about the fun morning and the bountiful gathering, as Cougar stripped off her bow and quiver, sat it aside and reached for her little boy, anxious to nurse the little one.

Squirrel had been roused by the whimpering of Bobcat and now she was fidgety and pursing her lips as she would when she was hungry and searching for a nipple. Dove grinned, and readied herself for the task, took the little one from the cradleboard and brought her to her breast. The women made themselves comfortable, sitting on the grass and leaning against the big boulder, enjoying the intimate moment with their infants.

Cougar finished nursing Bobcat, held him close and rocked him a little, staring at his features and smiling proudly at her firstborn. Reluctantly she reached for the cradleboard and began securing the infant in the apparatus. Dove also finished and was reaching for her cradle board, when the women heard a disturbance at the far edge of the brush, they instantly recognized the huffing and grunting of a bear. Cougar slowly stood to look over the top of the berry bushes. At the edge where she had already taken many of the berries, she saw the hump and brown fur of a grizzly.

Cougar slowly dropped below the brush, looked wide-eyed at Dove, and whispered, "Hurry, it's a grizzly. He's eating the berries, but he will probably smell us soon." Cougar went to her knees and reached for the cradleboard with Bobcat. Twisting and turning, she put the cradleboard on her back, then reached for her bow and quiver.

Dove quickly replaced Squirrel, motioned Chipmunk close, then put her cradleboard on her back, and snatched up her rifle. She checked the priming and snapped the frizzen down as quietly as possible. The women slowly stood, and the sudden crashing of the brush told them the grizzly had discovered them and was coming in a hurry to at least get a better look. Cougar nocked an arrow, motioned for Dove to grab Chipmunk, and start for the cabin. Dove grabbed the boy's hand, held her rifle in the other and started for the cabin as fast as the little boy's legs allowed.

31 / CHARGE

It was a restless night for the men, thoughts of the soon reunion with their wives and children filled their impatient minds as they fought their blankets in the darkness. The only one that seemed to be sleeping soundly was Wolf, who had been filled with wanderlust the previous nights and now slept with a contented restfulness. The waning moon was just past midpoint in the starlit sky when a frustrated Gabe kicked off the blankets and sat up, looking around the camp. A quick glance showed Wolf at his side, face between his paws, and unmoving. The horses stood hipshot with the silvery moon shadowing their backs with the tall ponderosa. Ezra flipped to his side, mumbling, either in his sleep or because of his restlessness. Gabe rose, stirred the coals, and lifted the coffeepot to judge its contents, but his shoulders slumped when he felt an empty pot. He stood, walked to the trickle of a creek, and rinsed out the pot and refilled it, returned to the fire, and sat the pot near.

"You too, huh?" growled the gravelly voiced Ezra, still under his blankets.

"Yeah, can't tell if it's just bein' anxious about gettin' home, or somethin' else," answered Gabe.

"Somethin' else?" queried Ezra.

"You know, like those premonitions you always get?"

"Yeah, but I ain't felt nothin'."

Gabe pushed the coffeepot a little closer, lifted his eyes to the sky and judged the time to be an hour or two past midnight. He looked back to Ezra, "Think you can get any more sleep?"

"More? Ain't hardly got any, so far. But no, I doubt if I could sleep or even rest." He looked around, saw Wolf lazily coming to his feet and stretching out, dropping his chest low as his hips stood tall as he strained back. Ezra glanced to the horses, saw Ebony turned back and looking at the men by the fire as if to say, "Well, you coming?"

Ezra rolled out of the blankets, went to his knees, and rolled up his blankets and ground cover, tied them tight and tossed the roll to the stack of gear beneath the ponderosa. He stood and went to the fire for his morning coffee and plopped down on the grey log beside the fire. He looked at Gabe, "So, you thinkin' we'll just head out, or do you wanna have breakfast first?"

"I figger to get a fistful of smoked meat to eat as we go, after we have our coffee of course."

Ezra nodded, reached for the pot to put in a handful of coffee, ground the night before, and replaced the pot beside the flames. They wasted little time downing the coffee and rigging the horses and with Wolf in the lead, they resumed their homeward trek north, following the flat-bottomed valley that was thick with tall green grass and willows that shadowed the meandering creek. The trail hung in the shadow of the alluvial shoulders that lay below the tall mountains to the east. The long barren slopes stretched about a mile to the timbered hillsides of the taller mountains, a few with bald granite peaks that clung to the recent snows. The cool air whispered down from those peaks and made Gabe and Ezra lift their collars and pull down their felt hats.

They were making good time, the horses seeming to sense they were homeward bound, and they stretched out. The pack animals were following free of lead ropes yet staying close behind the mounted horses. The sun had just topped the eastern peaks when they came to the mouth of the valley at the edge of the Big Hole Basin. The flat land was crowded with scattered timber, but when they came to the edge of the trees, they pushed into the warm sunshine and stopped beside the wide but shallow creek they had followed from the foothills. The men stepped down, let the horses and mule drink deep, then took their turn as they dipped the ice-cold clear water, drinking deep then splashing their faces for a refreshing wake-up. The men loosened the girths and let the animals graze a bit and get their wind while the men and Wolf stretched out in the soft grass and soaked up some sunshine.

"Not far now," offered Gabe.

"Nope. What you figger, two, three hours?" answered Ezra.

"Bout that." He paused, "What you reckon the women are doin' 'bout now?"

Ezra chuckled, "Prob'ly sittin' on the porch, drinkin' coffee and watchin' the young'uns scamper about. The little ones'll be rollin' on a blanket or buffalo robe and Chipmunk will be explorin' where he shouldn't be."

Both men chuckled at the image, then sat up, watching the animals snatch mouthfuls of grass, then lift their heads and look around, often looking back at the men. Wolf trotted to Ebony's side, flopped down on his belly, then rolled in the cool grass, and looked back at the men. All the animals appeared to be ready to move out, so the men looked at one another, shrugged and came to their feet.

As they came into the basin, they turned to the northwest, seeing the familiar line of snow-capped peaks that rose high above the black timbered shoulders whose foothills draped into the basin like the wide flowing skirt of a fancy ball gown. This was their homeland and the cabin, and their families, were just a couple hours away. The horses stepped out; heads high as they recognized the land as well. The sun hung in the clear sky, just over and slightly behind their right shoulders, the warmth felt good on their backs. Ezra started humming the familiar tune from his childhood in church, *Amazing Grace.* Gabe grinned as he listened, remembering his own times in church, and hearing the now popular tune and began singing the words as Ezra hummed the tune.

Amazing Grace, how sweet the sound,
That saved a wretch like me.
I once was lost, but now am found,
Was blind but now I see.

Both men laughed as they finished the song, looked at one another grinning and Ezra said, "It's a good thing we're not in church! They'd prob'ly throw us out after that!"

They had come to the mouth of their valley, and eagerly took the trail into the trees that led over the slight rise at the end of the eastern ridge. As they wound through the trees, Ezra frowned, looking around, then called ahead to Gabe, "Kick it up a little, I'm thinkin' we need to hurry!"

Gabe didn't question his friend, for he had been feeling uneasy all morning, and now that Ezra's senses confirmed it, this was not a time to hesitate. He slapped his legs to Ebony's side and kicked him into a canter, weaving through the trees, ducking low branches, and trying to see through the thick pines. They broke from the trees into the open mouth of the valley, but saw nothing and pushed the horses harder, kicking them into a gallop as the trail turned up the valley toward the lake that lay below the cabin. But nothing showed, and yet the men lay low on the necks of the charging animals, unconsciously reaching for their rifles and bringing them from the scabbards to the pommels.

Dove had started from the big boulder, telling Chipmunk, "Run, boy, run. Run to the cabin!" She tried to keep the fear from her voice, but the boy turned, eyes wide and fearful. As he turned back to his mother, he stumbled and fell backwards. Dove reached for him, dropping the parfleche, but stumbled herself and went to her knees. She turned, lifting the rifle, thinking the bear was about to pounce. She saw the brown bruin crashing through the brush, slapping it aside and he snapped his jaws with a clattering sound that was unmistakable of a hungry and angry grizzly. She stood, eared back the hammer, and brought the sights in line with the head of the beast, then lowered the sights to the side of the bear's neck. She caught a glimpse of Cougar Woman, standing tall and drawing her bow, but Dove focused on her sight and squeezed the trigger.

A tuft of hair and dust rose from the shoulder, the bear jerking his head around to see what varmint had bit him, but turned back and rose on his hind feet, head cocked to the side and mouth wide as he let loose a rumbling roar that bounced off the valley walls and echoed back. Dove looked down at Chipmunk who had scrambled to his feet and grabbed hold of his momma's leggings, then started to reload, but realized she had left the possibles pouch with the bullets in the cabin. She looked frantically at Cougar, saw her let the first arrow fly and watched it strike just under the standing bear's uplifted leg. The bear snarled, slapped at the nuisance, and turned toward Cougar.

Cougar nocked another arrow, sent it flying and watched as it struck the bear near the first arrow, and saw the bear drop to all fours, roar, and start a charge directly for Cougar. She hunkered below the level of the brush and started running toward Dove, motioning her to run to the trees. As she ran, she nocked another arrow, feeling the weight of the cradleboard at her back and fearful for the infant. She could not let the bear get to her and the child and was determined to do whatever it took to save her firstborn.

The racketing sound of a rifle charge rippled through the valley and sent a frightening jolt through the men. If the women were shooting, something was *definitely* wrong. Gabe slapped legs to Ebony, lying low on his neck and shouting for him to move faster. As he rounded the north bank of the lake, he saw the frantic Dove, trying to run, dragging Chipmunk behind. Then he saw Cougar, also running toward him, cradleboard bouncing at her back. But behind her, a massive grizzly just thrashed through the brush, stood on hind feet to search for his quarry. Gabe saw a black streak fly past Cougar, dug heels to Ebony, and took to the shallow water, avoiding the trail in the brush and cutting across the arm of the lake. Wolf struck the bear, but was slapped aside, and rolled in the brush.

Cougar saw Gabe coming, turned as she ran and shouted, pointing to the grizzly. Gabe slapped legs to Ebony, who lunged through the shallows, splashing water high and found solid footing at the shore. Gabe jammed both saddle pistols into his belt, leaped from the big stallion, landing at a run and lifted his rifle to his shoulder, earing back the hammer as he did, a quick aim, and he squeezed the trigger. The big Ferguson bucked, roared, and spat smoke and lead. Gabe squinted through the smoke, saw the bullet strike the bear's chest and watched the bear flinch, slap at the impact, and drop to all fours with a brush moving roar and started his leaping charge, snarling, growling, and snapping his jaws.

Gabe dropped his rifle, grabbed both saddle pistols,

cocking both hammers on each pistol and waited, a moment, more, until he saw the massive head and jowls fill his vision, and he pulled triggers. The pistols bucked, Gabe's fingers went to the rear triggers and pulled, again the pistols bucked, and smoke obscured his vision. Suddenly he felt the impact of the charging beast take him to his back and he snatched for his knife as he fell. But the weight of the massive beast pinned him underneath, and Gabe felt the monster moving, snapping his jaws, as he lifted his head, drool dropping on Gabe's face, and the bear snarled, mouth wide, and Gabe heard the bark of another rifle, Ezra!

The beast jerked, and rolled a little to the side, but Gabe still could not move. He felt something hot and wet against his chest, felt the monster breathe and heard the rattle in his chest as he fought for air, but then the big bruin lay still, and Gabe fought for breath of his own. Another blast sounded, he felt the beast jerk, but there was no other movement. Then he heard the voice of his friend, "Gabe? Gabe? Can you hear me?"

"Uhnn ... yeaaahh ... get this thing off me! I can't breathe!"

32 / WELCOME HOME

Ezra stood, looking for the women, saw both coming toward him, and motioned them to hurry. Cougar Woman ran to the bear, saw Gabe underneath, and immediately started pushing on the carcass. The cradleboard rocked on her back as she dug in her toes, buried her hands in the thick fur and pushed with her legs and arms for all she was worth. Dove quickly joined Ezra as each one grabbed a massive paw and pulled, trying to roll the monster off their friend.

Gabe grunted, struggled for breath, and tried to push with his one arm that was not pinned to his side. Wolf sunk his teeth into the hide of the beast and leaned back, digging with his paws, trying to help Ezra and Dove. Ezra let up, then said, "When I say, let's pull together! Now!" and everyone dug deeper, pushing, and pulling harder, until the beast started to roll. Cougar reached for Gabe's hand and pulled, dragging his torso from under the behemoth. Ezra, Dove, and Wolf continued to pull against the massive weight while Cougar pulled and now Gabe pushed, and the man was finally freed. He dropped to his back, sucking air, and wincing as he grabbed his side. Ezra dropped to his haunches, muttered, "That woulda been a lot easier if he weren't so weighted down with lead!" He paused, thinking, counting with his fingers, "Let's see," nodding to Dove, "You shot him once, Cougar put two arrows in him, Gabe shot him, uh, five times, once with the rifle and all four barrels of the pistols. Then I shot him with my rifle and gave the coup de grâce with my pistol. So, that's eight balls of lead and two arrows! No wonder he was hard to move!" Gabe chuckled, grunted and Cougar moved closer, touching him tenderly, looking at the cuts and frowned, "Did he do this?" pointing at his skull. The hat and bandage had come off and his scalp wound showed.

Gabe tried to laugh but winced at the pain in his chest from the crushing weight of the bear and shook his head slightly, "No," he grunted, "That...w.. w ..was when the ...buffalo ran . . . me over." He let the rest of his air escape and his chest fell, then he drew deeply of the mountain air, and forced a smile at Cougar and reached for her. She frowned, shook her head, and pulled him close and they embraced. He grunted, pushed away, and struggled to stand.

Cougar helped him to his feet, held on to him to steady him, and pulled him close again. With her arms wrapped around his neck, his around her waist, she leaned back and said, "And what else happened while you were gone?"

Gabe glanced at Ezra who was hugging on his wife, his son tugging on his trousers, and the men grinned as Gabe said, "We'll tell you all about it when we get to the cabin."

With four knives working, they made short work of skinning the big grizzly. The meat would be saved but would not be their choice for eating. The bear fat, however, had many purposes and would be put to good use. As they stripped the hide from legs, Dove cut away the long claws, glanced at Ezra, "Now you will have a claw necklace like Spirit Bear!"

Gabe sat on his haunches, looked at the women and the toddler that was sitting beside Ezra. He glanced at the two cradleboards that stood against the boulder, the little ones' heads shaded with the overhanging cover, and smiled. He looked at Cougar, "How 'bout Ezra and I finish up with the bear, and you ladies take the little ones and the pack animals to the cabin. We'll be along shortly and unload the horses and come back for this," pointing at the carcass with his chin. "Ain't nothin' gonna get close enough to the bear smell to start chewin' on him 'fore we get back anyway."

"Or you could come with us now, and come after

that later," suggested a smiling Cougar. "We will fix a good meal for you, since you have been gone so long and forgot what good cooking was like!"

The men looked at one another, shrugged, and stood. They caught up the horses, whistled for the pack animals, and the two couples started to the trail that would take them to the cabin. Ezra and Dove led the way, walking beside one another, Dove leading Ezra's bay and with the mule following. Ezra had Chipmunk on his shoulders as he dug his fingers in his father's hair, making Ezra grimace ever so often, to the laughter of both Dove and Chipmunk.

Gabe and Cougar Woman sided one another, hands clasped together, Gabe's free hand trailing the reins of Ebony as Wolf walked beside Cougar. The grey pack horse plodding close behind the black stallion. Gabe still favored his bad ankle and occasionally grabbed at his ribs as the stabbing pain from his previous injury had been compounded by the crushing weight of the bear, and he knew there were either more ribs cracked, or broken.

Cougar had watched as her husband struggled, offered her shoulder for him to lean on but he just frowned and shook his head. She noticed he was slightly bent over, favoring his ribs, and limping on one leg. "When we get to the cabin, I want to look you over for all your injuries. You need tending."

Gabe shook his head a little, looked sideways

at his woman, and with a bit of a smile, answered, "You won't get any argument out of me on that count. As I think about it, I don't know of anything that *doesn't* hurt."

"It could have been worse. That grizzly's teeth were this close," she held out her thumb and forefinger, about three inches apart, "to your face!"

"I know. I smelled his breath! Whhooooee!"

Cougar laughed, looked at her man and smiled, "It is good you are home," she declared, leaning her head to his shoulder.

They were soon at the clearing before the cabin and Ezra paused, looking at their home and the surroundings. Gabe and Cougar came alongside, glanced at Ezra, and looked at the cabin, and said, "Look's good, don't it?"

"Mighty good," answered Ezra.

"Come on you two, there's work to do!" declared a grinning Dove, starting out for the cabin. As they approached the steps, the men moved to the side, and tethered the horses to unload the gear and meat that would go in the house or the store room behind. They dropped the packs, panniers, and parfleches at the foot of the stairs, then started to the corral and shed to strip the animals. The women mounted the steps and went into the cabin, Wolf trotting behind.

Gabe opened the pole gate, held it while Ezra led his bay and the mule in, the grey pack horse trailing behind, then followed with Ebony. As they stripped the saddles from their horses, Ezra looked at Gabe, "You know we won't get a horse near that bear, don'tchu?"

"The mule might, he doesn't seem to be afraid of much of anything."

"Yeah, maybe. We'll just have to try and see. Maybe tether him away, then we can debone the meat and fat, roll up the hide, and haul it to him. That might work."

"Maybe," resolved Gabe, putting the saddles and pack saddles and other tack in the shed.

"But right now, I'm so hungry, my belly button's pinchin' muh backbone!" declared Ezra.

The women had prepared a fine meal for their family, broiled buffalo steaks, vegetables including potatoes, camas bulbs, and roasted piñon nuts, fresh biscuits and mixed berries. The men were smiling and enjoying everything as the women enjoyed the company of their men. Chipmunk sat atop a single bound volume of combined works by Thomas Paine as he sat on the bench beside his daddy. The men sat back, lifted their coffee cups in a toast to the women as Gabe said, "Ladies, we salute you! Excellent meal!"

"Hear, hear!" added Ezra, much to the delight of the womenfolk.

"So, now you can tell us what happened while you were gone," suggested Cougar, leaning her elbows on the table after pushing aside the plates.

Dove leaned forward also, and Gabe glanced to Ezra, who shrugged, and Gabe began, "Well, the trip down was uneventful, except for the bear, but that was nothing. But when we got into the valley before the Snake River plains, we came on a village of Paiute that were massacred by some *Waiilatpus...*" and he continued to tell about the Paiute and the Waiilatpus, and was thrilled in the telling about the Spirit Dance and the rattlesnakes, which brought a lot of laughter from the women.

As the laughter ebbed, Gabe nodded to Ezra, "And I'll let Bonecrusher tell the next part."

"Bonecrusher?" asked Dove.

Ezra grinned and began to tell of their visit to the Paiute village, the fight with the raiders, and how he earned the name of the legend of the Paiute. He continued to talk and spoke about the bread bugs, but was stopped by Dove, "You mean crickets?"

Ezra frowned, nodding, and glanced from Dove to Cougar, then grinned. "Yup, brought you some too! They're in the parfleche yonder, next to the one with the piñon nuts."

The women smiled and went to the parfleches to find the treasure, finding one of camas bulbs also. They were more thrilled than a white woman getting a new store-bought dress, and both hugged their men before sitting to hear the rest of the story.

Gabe picked up and started with the buffalo hunt,

but was interrupted by Cougar, "Oh, you mean the real reason you left us and went there?"

"Uh, yeah," and he continued to relate about the buffalo hunt, the attempt by Tauitau to drive the bull into him, and how he was trampled by the stragglers. Cougar frowned, feeling his pain as he tumbled under the stampeding buffalo, but urged him to continue. "So, we went after him, got my rifle back, and came home!"

The women looked at one another, shook their heads and laughed. Cougar said to Dove, "We just cannot trust them alone. Next time, they can stay with the children and we will go hunt!"

The women rose and went to the side of their seated men and pulled their heads against them, running their fingers through their hair. Gabe lay his head against the waist of Cougar, frowned, and put his hand on her tummy, leaned back and looked, his hand resting at her waist, then lifted his eyes to her and asked, "What's this?" She looked down at him and smiled, that familiar mischievous glint in her eye, and let the smile answer his question.

A LOOK AT: TO KEEP A PROMISE

The power of a promise made and a promise kept is realized when Jeremiah Thompsett comes of age and accepts the responsibility of fulfilling his mentor's long-held dream. Raised by an escaped slave in the midst of the Arapaho nation in the Wind River mountains, he now must track down the slave catchers that killed his adopted father and stole their cache. The Vengeance Quest takes him and his companions through the mountains and across the nation to fulfill the promise of freeing the family of slaves held dear to his mentor and adopted father.

Accompanied by Broken Shield and Laughing Waters, his Arapaho friend and his sister, the trek through the mountains and to Fort Union is fraught with hazard and ambush. It is here he is joined by Scratch, the crusty mountain man who joins him on his journey downriver and across country to find Ezekiel's family and to seek to free them.

AVAILABLE NOW

ABOUT THE AUTHOR

Born and raised in Colorado into a family of ranchers and cowboys, B.N. Rundell is the youngest of seven sons. Juggling bull riding, skiing, and high school, graduation was a launching pad for a hitch in the Army Paratroopers. After the army, he finished his college education in Springfield, MO, and together with his wife and growing family, entered the ministry as a Baptist preacher.

Together, B.N. and Dawn raised four girls that are now married and have made them proud grandparents. With many years as a successful pastor and educator, he retired from the ministry and followed in the footsteps of his entrepreneurial father and started a successful insurance agency, which is now in the hands of his trusted nephew. He has also been a successful audiobook narrator and has recorded many books for several award-winning authors. Now finally realizing his life-long dream, B.N. has turned his efforts to writing a variety of books, from children's picture books and young adult adventure books, to the historical fiction and western genres.

Printed in Great Britain
by Amazon